BOB KELLY

CHICAGO DETECTIVE JACK FALLON IN THE MYSTERY OF LEGALLY DEAD

Dedication

This book is dedicated to my grandmother, Mary Cogan who was a parent of me and my brother Andy. She inspired us with her dignity and fortitude.

Acknowledgment

Thanks to Morgan Beldock for her technical support. Thanks to Ebbe Salling for proofreading. Thanks to Jenna Moudy for her artistic inspiration.

Table of Contents

Chapter 1

I woke up on a beautiful sunny morning the Thursday before Labor Day. I threw on some shorts, a white Bears T-shirt and running shoes. Looking out my front room windows, I could see Lincoln Park behind the buildings on N. Clarendon Ave. Summer in Chicago was still in full swing, and I was eager to get out into it.

After an elevator ride down from the 12th floor, I walked briskly out the front door waving to Benny behind the entrance security desk and bolted out onto the street for my run. I had several routes and decided on a 4 mile jaunt which took me largely through some of the paths in the park eventually reaching the lake and then along it for a while before going back through Lincoln Park and crossing North Clarendon and back home.

The temperature was already in the 70s, and the air was moist. I quickly broke a sweat and started slowly, taking into consideration the pedestrians and traffic on the streets. When I got to the park, I picked up the pace and decided to push myself, until I got near Montrose and then opened it up, until I hit the beach and got to the water. My heart was pounding. and my lungs were burning.

The cool breezes off Lake Michigan were welcome and helped me recover, as I walked along the shore enjoying the wide open vista of our inland ocean. There were some swimmers and a few kayakers just off the shore and some small sailboats further out. I continued going south along the shoreline, until I cut back across the beach to a path leading into the park joining other walkers, runners and bicyclists and hit a moderate pace all the way home.

Once back in my 12th floor apartment, I peeled off the soaking T-shirt and shorts and hit the shower. I enjoyed the cleansing wash and cold blast that followed to get me focused. It was technically a day off, but in the world of the detective there was really no such thing. We are always on call either formally or informally. Or, as was the case this day, I was going to court to testify in a three year old case that was the result of arrests made, while I was a new detective and partnered with veteran Vernon Johnson.

Consequently, I would be heading to our iconic courthouse at 26th and California. My current partner Elaina Rodriguez had plans to spend the day in Pilsen with her little girls, Rosie and Lucy, and I hoped that she would be able to enjoy it without getting called in.

After a light breakfast of orange juice, Catherine Clark's wheat toast and frosted flakes I donned some khaki slacks, short-sleeved Oxford blue button-down shirt, a green tie with gold stripes and a tan sport coat over my holster carrying my Beretta. My star went on my brown belt, and I slipped on some brown Rockport walking shoes over tan socks.

The elevator carried me down to the parking area, and I hopped into my black on black Chevy Camaro convertible and made my way out onto North Clarendon and then east to Dusable Lakeshore Drive. I took it going south beginning along Lincoln Park near where my run had taken me and enjoyed the view of the lake, as I contemplated the main focus of my work for that day.

I was scheduled to testify in the murder trial of the young guy from North Lawndale named William {Billy} Sims. I had arrested him after my partner Vernon Johnson and I had been called out to check on a report of a possible assault and robbery going on at an apartment building in River North.

When we arrived at the apartment building, the information was that screams were heard coming from apartment 310 and that two young black men had been seen leaving the building shortly before we arrived. Vernon Johnson was the senior partner and took charge. He told me to pull over right behind a parked older model gold Buick Regal. We saw a young black guy coming from the sidewalk near the front entrance and walking toward the Buick.

Johnson told me to check the guy out. He was going into the building. Just then a squad car pulled up, and he told the uniformed officer to follow him.

By this time the young guy just reached the driver side of the Regal. I approached him and announced that I was Chicago PD and flashed the star on my belt. He continued to open the car door, and I ordered him to stop and he did, but his posture and the scowl on his face put me on alert.

I asked him for his name and ID. He was now partially behind the open door and I moved around him to get a better view and put myself in a position to prevent him from jumping into the car. At that time another patrol car pulled up, and I glanced at the officers exiting their car. At that moment the kid punched me in the left side of my face and tried to jump into the driver seat. Before he could get the key in the old Buick, I recovered and grabbed him by the collar of his black T-shirt and pulled him out onto the road.

This guy was agile and he quickly jumped up causing me to lose my grip on his shirt. He came right at me, but I sidestepped to his left and delivered a strong right hand punch to his left temple which staggered him. I grabbed his left arm and spun him around then slammed him face first on the hood of his car and put the cuffs on.

The two uniforms rushed over, and I told them to put him in their car and stay with him. I was going into the building. I hurried to the front entrance and as I did I caught a glimpse of a young black man at the end of the block walking normally and turning left at the corner. For a moment I thought about going after him, but I didn't know what my partner had walked into. I decided to go to apartment 310. The first arriving uniformed officers were outside keeping residents at a distance and asking them what they had seen and heard.

When I entered the apartment, Vernon Johnson was gingerly walking through the tidy space which seemed undisturbed except for a knocked over floor lamp and a young woman on the living room floor in a pool of blood. Johnson grimly told me that she was gone and that he had called for the crime scene team and the Medical Examiner's Office.

We stayed on the scene, until the CSI guys and the homicide detectives arrived. They took over, and we went back downstairs to our car. On the way out the door I noticed something in the bushes to my left near the front entrance. I knelt down and could see a long kitchen knife that seem to be covered in blood. I told one of the uniformed officers named Brady to get one of the CSI officers down here.

He came back with officer Carla Kravitz and Detective Thomas Deso. I told them that I had just spotted a knife in the bushes and pointed it out to them. We were going back to our station to book Billy Sims on assault and resisting arrest charges. They knew where to find us.

So that was the case I mulled over as I continued my journey down Lakeshore Drive past Monroe Harbor, the Buckingham Fountain, Soldier Field and McCormick Place before exiting at 26 Street and taking it all the way to 2650 S. California Ave. Before long I could see the iconic George N. Leighton Courthouse built in the 1920s.

I pulled into the secure parking lot across the street and showed my ID, and they checked my name with the witness list for the Williams Sims murder trial. I pulled into a spot and put the top up on the Camaro and put the windows up leaving a crack open on both. It was another hot summer day in the great city of Chicago.

I walked across California Avenue. Straight ahead was the imposing concrete Greek columned building with the big shoulders. I felt a surge of excitement and pride in anticipation of the culmination of one of my cases. A murder trial is the ultimate dramatic ending to a detective's hard work and the fulfillment of my boyhood dreams. I had always wanted to be on the right side of the law and to get the bad guys off the street.

Inside, the security line for police officers and lawyers wasn't too bad, especially compared to the long slow moving crowd of relatives, friends and curious onlookers, waiting to get in for one of the day's many trials scheduled in the thirty courtrooms.

Security at Chicago's most famous courthouse was handled by the Cook County Sheriff's Deputies who confiscated cell phones and cameras from first timers further slowing down the procession that by then had extended out onto the sidewalk.

I presented my ID and was informed that the trial of the People v William Sims was in Judge Kate Hogan's courtroom on the third floor. The first floor high ceilinged rotunda presented an image of impressive marbled history, elegance and dilapidation. The place was bustling with lawyers, detectives, uniformed cops and an amusing conglomeration of outfits worn by the throngs headed to the various morality plays scheduled for the day.

I walked up the stairs to the third floor and to courtroom 302. To the left of the entrance to room 302 I noticed my old partner Vernan Johnson standing in the hallway talking to a couple of prosecutors that I recognized as Assistant State's Attorneys Mark Fortuna and Paige Owira.

Vernon Johnson waived me over. and I approached them as other attorneys and onlookers buzzed by us. We exchanged greetings and Vernon gave a warm handshake saying it was good to see me. I reciprocated, and we kept it short promising to catch up later. We both new that we had a serious job ahead of us. Attorney Fortuna took Vernan by the arm and said they needed to prep us for testimony separately.

I remained in place with Attorney Owira whom I had met previously at the State's Attorney's Office at 69 W. Washington Street downtown. She was a strikingly beautiful woman with dark brown hair, light brown skin and sparkling hazel eyes. Her conservative lawyers outfit was unable to disguise an amazing figure. But, her stern professional manner made it a little easier to concentrate on the reason for me being there.

She was aware of my prepared statement and police report and that I had already been prepped for testifying. So, she just gave me an outline of how the morning would go. The prosecution had already put on two days of evidence and testimony for their case. My former partner and I were their last two witnesses and Vernan

Johnson would be called first. She didn't expect either of us to take too long on direct or cross examination since neither one of us had witnessed the murder. I would go last since I had had the altercation with the defendant and made the arrest.

We went over how Detective Johnson and I were called to the apartment building and my encounter with Sims and how I later spotted the knife in the bushes while exiting the building. Just then, another dark suited prosecutor named Terrance Goggins approached us and asked Paige Owira to go checkon how Mark Fortuna was doing with Detective Johnson.

I thought this was strange and unnecessary. And, frankly I hated to see her leave. He said wanted to go over my timeline again. When I mentioned that Attorney Owira had just done that, Goggins kind of smirked and informed me that he was the lead prosecutor in the case and that he would be handling my direct examination. Ok I thought. It's your show. Go for it.

I didn't like Goggins. He was overly confident which came across as being more cocky than competent. He was around forty and in good shape at six feet 180 pounds. He was dressed to the hilt in a black Italian made suit, gray shirt, maroon tie with a ruby studded tie pin and a maroon accent kerchief in his breast pocket. A bit of a dandy I thought to myself.

So, I went over the timeline again without interruption until I got to the part where I exited the apartment building after going inside to meet up with my partner. At that point Goggins lowered his voice almost to a whisper and asked me, "Is this where you found the knife inside the car?"

I was taken aback. "No." I responded. "Didn't you read my report?" I exclaimed.

He motioned for me to keep my voice down and whispered, "Are you absolutely sure you didn't make a mistake in your report? This is an important case for me and it could be for you too. It would look pretty damn bad for both of us, if this low life walks because you got your facts mixed up. You follow me?"

I looked hard into his green eyes and said, "Yeah, I follow you alright, but I don't like where you're going. I'm going to forget what you just said and chalk it up to you getting your facts mixed up."

At that moment a court officer informed us that Judge Hogan was getting ready to take the bench. Prosecutor Goggins didn't bat an eye. He went back to his usual voice level and told me to wait out in the hall, until I was called. After my testimony concluded, I was free to remain in the courtroom.

He turned and Paige accompanied him into courtroom 302. I knew the drill after testifying in six or seven trials and having watched my dad in action several times during high school and college. He was a great trial lawyer and, in fact, was involved in a trial that day on the fourth floor. Every time I underwent cross examination, I was glad that it wasn't defense attorney Ed Fallon asking the questions. It wasn't just because he was a terrific lawyer. It was more that I knew that visions of him getting the truth out of me as a kid would be replaying in my head.

The wait gave me time to think about the case against Billy Sims. On the one hand, he had assaulted me and had a couple of previous convictions for assault and battery. There was no doubt that he had a temper and was capable of acting out. He was at the scene and seemed to have had the opportunity to commit the murder. On the other hand, the prosecution was unable to find any connection between the victim and Sims. The only identifiable DNA on the bloody knife was that of the victim, Jemina Jones. Also, there were none of Sims fingerprints or DNA found in her apartment. There were, however, prints and male DNA from unknown people. But, since Jemina was a popular young woman with an active social life which included hosting parties, it didn't seem surprising that there would be unidentified prints and DNA at her place. No wonder Goggins was worried, I thought.

After about 45 minutes the courtroom door opened, Vernon Johnson walked out and he was not smiling. He gave me a nod and simply said "take care of yourself in there, Jack."

I nodded in return and told my old partner that I intended to, and that it was great to see him. A court officer escorted me into courtroom 302. It seemed even warmer and stuffier than the hallway. Billy Sims was seated at the defense table flanked by two female attorneys, one of whom I recognized as Linda Prassas from the Public Defender's Office. The tall slender attorney somewhere in her forties was experienced with a good reputation in the criminal defense world. She was one of my dad's favorites.

Terrance Goggins called out that the prosecution called Detective Jack Fallon. I walked up to the witness stand to the left of Judge Kate Hogan who sat high above everyone in a throne like large leather chair. After being sworn in, I sat down in the wooden chair in the witness box.

Prosecutor Goggins lead me through the usual introductory routine and the step by step details of how Detective Johnson and I got to the apartment building and what happened afterward. The questions proceeded as I expected with few objections from the defense, and those that were made got denied by Judge Hogan.

When it came to how and when I found the bloody knife, he simply asked me if I found anything at the scene outside the apartment building and whether Billy Sims car was nearby. I thought that was clever, since I could answer yes without specifically saying where exactly it was found, while leaving the impression that it was near the car and connected to Billy Sims. Clever I thought but a little sleezy. I wondered whether Linda Prassas had noticed.

She did. After Goggins finished with me, Defense Attorney Linda Prassas couldn't wait to get started with her cross examination. She had me state exactly where I had found the knife in the bushes, and then she concentrated on everything that I hadn't seen. She had a whole litany of question, all of which I had to answer "no." Hell, I hadn't even seen Sims come out of the apartment building. The best I could do was to say that he had been on the sidewalk outside the building, before I confronted him at his car.

When she was finished with me, Goggins declined to redirect examine me and announced that the prosecution rested. I was told that I was free to go but could stay since my testimony had concluded. The judge instructed the Defense to call its first witness, so I decided to stay awhile.

The defense lawyers and Sims huddled in hushed but animated voices with the table microphones muted. After a few minutes Judge Hogan told Linda Prassas to proceed in no uncertain terms. After another couple of minutes of seemingly intense discussion, Prassas turned her microphone back on and called William Sims to the stand.

I could tell that Linda Prassas was not happy. Outwardly she did her best to present a good poker face, but her body language and the look on her co-counsel's face said otherwise She calmly walked Sims through his actions on the day in question. He did ok on direct examination and explained that he was unfamiliar with the River North neighborhood. He had gone there looking for a party that a friend of his had told him about the day before. He had the address right, but ended up on the wrong street. Consequently, he had turned around and was walking back to his car when he didn't see the name he was looking for on any of the mail boxes in the lobby. It was then that the pushy cop {meaning me} confronted him, and he thought he was just being hassled because he was a black guy in a mostly white neighborhood.

At the Prosecutor's table I saw Terrance Goggins posture stiffen, as he leaned over to say something to Paige Owira. Now he seemed to be the one who couldn't wait to get going on his cross examination. So, after Attorney Prassas finished up her direct examination he jumped into action.

Goggins began peppering Sims with questions while waving his arms dramatically and walking right up to the defendant and then turning his back on him and walking back to the Prosecution table while prancing around the courtroom still asking questions and smirking at Sim's answers. The tactics seemed to unnerve the young defendant. He couldn't remember the name of the friend that invited him to the party. He only knew that the guy was known on the street as JJ. He didn't know where JJ lived, if he had a job or any family in Sim's North Lawndale neighborhood.

Goggins did a great job of twisting "done with this guy" Billy Sims into a pretzel, and it was clearly getting to him. Then all of a sudden everything went haywire. The prosecutor was once again walking right up to the defendant getting within inches of his face. He told the Judge that he was "done with this guy". Then, when Judge Hogan looked down at her witness list, Goggins turned his back to the jury and seemed to mouth something.

Billy Sims roared out something that was not understandable to me and lept out of the witness box and onto Terrance Goggins back. They both tumbled to the floor exchanging punches until court officers waded into the brawls, separated the two and place handcuffs on Sims.

The Judge was flabbergasted and struggled to find her gavel. She pounded it hard several times while ordering the crowd to come to order and remain in their seats. She then excused the jury and recessed the trial until 9:30AM the next day.

What in the hell was that!

Chapter 2

After the jury and the defendant were ushered out of the courtroom, I remained in my seat in the gallery watching the stunned crowd file out. One of the court officers, a young woman with jet black short cropped hair, approached me with a serious perturbed look on her face.

I pulled my jacket back exposing the star on my belt, but her expression didn't change much. She was thoroughly unimpressed and said that she knew who I was and had seen me testify, but that I still had to leave. I wasn't really surprised. Chicago court officers don't get surprised or impressed by much. And, the deputies that work 26th and Cal see a parade of high-powered lawyers, mobsters and detectives as well as the worst sort of violent criminals every damn day. Business as usual to them.

I stood up and slowly began walking out, when I nearly bumped into prosecutor, Paige Owira who had gathered her briefcase and a box full of files after the melee. She had her head down seemingly deep in thought, and my mind was wandering around with thoughts of what had just happened and what I was going to do with the rest of my day.

When Paige looked up, we were only inches away from each other, and I couldn't help feeling an intense physical attraction. The grim look on her face softened a little, and she almost smiled saying, "oh sorry Detective Fallon. I am a little bit preoccupied right now."

"I can imagine." I said. "Do you know what the fiasco was all about?"

"Not really," she responded. "We knew that Sims was a hothead and that he could probably get him to look bad on the stand, but I never imagined something like that."

"I would really like to talk to you more about this case sometime. I am a little confused about some things." I said.

Owira stopped and looked back at me. "Another time detective. I have my hands full in more ways than one at the moment."

I nodded, and she walked briskly out of the courtroom which seemed totally hollow in her absence. The stuffy humid air now seemed more oppressive, and I felt the need to get away from courtroom 302.

The stairs lead down to the marble floored lobby, and I decided to go to the old first floor cafeteria to gather my thoughts. I sauntered down the sweltering hallway feeling repulsed and compelled to stay at the same time. I needed to remain and experience more of this challenging historic Hall of Justice. The justice part was weighing heavily on my mind in a way that it never had before.

I picked up a tray and went through the line and ordered a bowl of chili and a Coke. I found the last table in the back. I didn't want any company. I sat down and started in on my chili and immediately broke out into a full sweat. Holy moly it was spicy as hell and hot! The cold Coke helped a little along with some crackers. The best thing was that it took my mind in a different direction.

The lunch break must have begun since the archaic cafeteria room filled up in a couple of minutes. The crowd was an astonishing collection of finely tailored suits, uniforms, and casual poverty. It was Chicago in microcosm. I tried the chili and crackers again with much the same result. While wiping sweat from my face with a napkin that was not nearly substantial enough for the job, I noticed a dark figure approaching my table at a brisk pace. I immediately regained my focus and recognized my former partner and friend, Vernon Johnson.

I stood up and greeted him motioning for him to sit down. He put his iced tea on the table and took a seat. It was great to see him, and he was just the person I needed at the moment. He had heard some rumblings about something weird going on in our case, but he didn't know what had actually happened. So, I told him about what went on in the courtroom and my exchanges with prosecutors Owira and Goggins.

Vernon Johnson leaned back in his chair and shot me a look that I saw so often in my rookie year as a detective."This is the kind of thing that black people have been dealing with for decades in Chicago Jack. Sometimes the anger just rises to the surface and erupts like a volcano. It isn't always about the right or wrong of a particular case. It just is."

Now I sat back in my chair. I spent nearly every day with Detective Johnson for three years and he had never talked about race, made excuses for black defendants or felt sorry for himself about growing up black in Chicago. His matter-of-fact statement made me feel uncomfortable. It made me question how much I really knew about how nearly 1/3 of the people living in our great city of Chicago experienced it on a daily basis. I couldn't say anything.

Vernon broke the silence. "Don't get me wrong Jack. The black community has plenty of problems and we need to face a lot of them head on in our families and neighborhoods. That is why I needed to go back to Austin to contribute to where I grew up. I will retire there or I will die there. But bad cases have been and continue to be brought against young black men in this city. That's just the way it is."

"Do you think the Sims case is one of those?" I sincerely wanted to know.

Johnson just shook his head a little and simply said, "I don't know but, it is not a very strong case in my opinion. Everything is very circumstantial at best. They could prove the kid is a hot hotheaded jerk even before he went after the prosecutor. and now the jury may not be able to see past that. All we can do is present our evidence and tell the truth, no matter what they want you to say."

That last sentence got my attention. "You mean you have seen this kind of thing before?" I asked.

Vernon raised an eyebrow and smiled wryly. "Yeah, I've seen it many times over the years."

"Did Goggins try to pressure you to change your testimony in this case?" I asked.

Not this time. He knows me now, and wouldn't have the balls to try it again. It is been good to see you Jack. I need to meet a CI in South Austin in a while, so got to go." He finished his iced tea, stood up and we shook hands as friends. When he walked away from the table, I felt a sense of pride in knowing such a man.

I had lost all interest in the firestorm chili and pushed it away. The Coke had lost all the ice in the nearly stifling air of the antiquated cafeteria, but still was cold enough for me to want one more gulp. The thought of trying to find my dad crossed my mind, but I knew that while he is in the middle of a trial he wouldn't be available. Even to me.

When I rose from the table, a cockroach the size of a mouse scurried across the center of the room and disappeared into the far wall. It was not my first cockroach siding at 26th and California, but the size was impressive. I couldn't help wondering how the mice were faring in their battle for dominance within the hallowed walls and halls of Chicago's most iconic courthouse.

Well, that was enough of that. I had been at 26th and California long enough for one day. So, I made my way down the hallway and through the marbled lobby and onto the street. It was out of the frying pan and into the fire of a blazing hot Chicago day. Walking across the street to the parking lot, the pavement seemed to be roiling causing a barrage of heat waves.

My black Camaro was like an oven left on overnight by mistake. I opened both doors and got in to start the engine and crank up the AC before exiting again and closing the doors. I needed to get my mind focused back on the job. There were other cases to solve including our newest one. It was the murder of 34-year-old Cheryl Greenberg outside of a restaurant in Streeterville.

A couple of minutes were long enough. I needed to get out of the sun and the heat regardless of how well my AC had cooled down the inside of my black on black Chevy Camaro. Inside it was lukewarm but the cool air was pouring through the vents and even cooling down the black leather seats.

I pulled out of the lot and headed north on California Avenue without knowing whether I was going home or someplace for a beer. Either way, I decided to take my time and stay on California Avenue and drive through Little Village and a few other neighborhoods on my way back to Uptown.

Everyone on the street seem to be moving in slow motion, sapped of strength by the oppressive dew point. I was starting to feel human, as my body temperature dropped. The sidewalks were less populated than usual, and those leaving the various businesses quickly got into their cars or went from one store to the next.

At Division Street I turned right and drove through the East Humboldt Park neighborhood toward Ukrainian Village. I hadn't been around there since before the Russian invasion and my desire for a beer was taking over. I remembered a little neighborhood place called Stella's Sports Bar on N. Western Avenue.

A right turn on Western and a short drive brought me to the corner dive bar.

When I walked into the small dark local with a well-worn pool table and unbacked barstools, the few regulars in the place turned to stare at the dude dressed like a cop. I was happy that I recognized the bartender, a 50 something bony woman with long dark hair streaked with gray and sharp facial features named Rita.

"Well if it isn't my long lost son Jack Fallon. How the hell have you been? What's with the suit?"

I realize that I may not have been in there since I made detective. When my buddies and I started going in the place during our days at DePaul, she referred to us as her kids. She knew we were under age but we behaved ourselves and usually lost at pool to the regulars.

She placed a Miller High Life in front of me and raised a bottle of Jack Daniels asking "One and one Jack?"

I smiled. "You're still amazing Rita. Glad to see you haven't lost your touch."

She poured a shot of Jack for me and one for herself. We clinked glasses and bolted them down. "It's good to see you again. How long has it been?"

"I'm not sure. Did you know that I made detective?"

"Hell no I didn't! Hey guys, "she announced to the four regulars sitting at the bar. "One of my kids did good! Everybody say hello to Detective Jack Fallon. Let's   have a shot!"

She poured Jack's for me and herself and the others happily took the same. They all raised their glasses to me and I reciprocated. Down they went and Rita turned on the jukebox and registered enough credits to last all day. I thoroughly enjoyed myself for a couple of hours before saying my goodbyes to Rita and the boys.

The searing heat hit me immediately. I'll say one thing for Stella's Sports Bar, the air conditioning is top-notch. Coming out of the dark man cave to the bright intense sunlight made it difficult to focus. I looked across Western Ave and spotted my Camaro a few yards across and up the street.

As I edged out onto the road, I noticed a young black kid of around 16 years old walking briskly across Western toward my side of the street. Normally, I wouldn't have thought anything of it except that he was wearing baggy gray pants and a blue hooded sweatshirt with the hood up. This piqued my interest.

The kid stopped in the street in front of a middle-aged lady wearing pink shorts and a white T-shirt. She had just opened the driver side door on her bright blue Toyota Camry. She glanced back at the guy and instinctively shifted her purse to her right hand and clutched it to her side.

The kid grabbed her left arm violently and spun her around causing her to be thrown backwards hitting the side of the car. She bounced off and fell to the pavement. The traffic on Western Avenue kept coming and cars and trucks were swerving around them and dangerously merging into the outside lane.

I started sprinting along the parked cars and yelled at the young guy to stop and stay put. At first, he stood his ground and appeared to be ready to take me on but when I announced that I was Chicago PD and got closer to him, I could see the expression on his face change to one of panic.

At that time a car horn blared and he turned to look across the street. I saw someone in a silver Ford F 150 motioned for him to join him. Whoever it was appeared to be a white guy in his 30s who had shaggy light brown hair wearing a black T-shirt and sunglasses.

The kid bolted out into the traffic narrowly avoiding a couple of SUVs. My instincts told me to go after the little bastard but the lady on the pavement let out a shrill cry for help, and I had to get her out of the road and checked out for injuries. So, I gingerly picked her up placing one hand under her back in the other under the back of her thighs.

I gently placed her on the sidewalk and looked up to see the silver pickup around 20 yards away speeding south on Western. I couldn't see anything from the license plate other than it was Illinois. My first call was to 911 for an ambulance and my second was to police dispatch asking for a bolo on the silver Ford F 150.

The victim was in pretty bad shape. She was able to give her name, René Mesirow, and her address in Irving Park. She was expressing a great deal of pain located in multiple places on her body but kept moaning that her arm was killing her. It was apparent that her left arm was limp and probably broken.

The ambulance was first to arrive and the response time was impressive. Before they took over, I was able to get her to answer a couple of quick questions. She had never seen her assailant before and said that he yelled at her to give him her key or he would kill her and called her a fucking bitch. When the EMTs came over, I backed away and let the professionals do their thing.

Then a couple of squad cars arrived immediately, followed by an unmarked car carrying a couple of detectives who were unfamiliar to me. They began barking orders at the uniformed officers in a way that seemed a little condescending, but their tone changed markedly when addressing me, after they clearly notice my detective star on my belt. They introduced themselves as Detective Oscar Anderson, a tall sandy haired guy in his mid-30s and Jorge Solar, a shorter stocky dark-haired man in his early 40s. They were part of the carjacking task force which was extensive with various units in all of Chicago's six major areas. Their unit covered all of Area 3 which included my Near North District, the Ukrainian Village and the surrounding neighborhoods. They worked out of the detective headquarters on W. Belmont Ave.

They took my full statement, and we exchanged our cards. I was just about to leave the scene when two more detectives pulled up got out and approached us. Anderson and Solar didn't wait for the new guys. They just walked to their white Impala and as Detective Anderson got into the driver side, he called out to the new arrivals.

"It's all yours. He's very cooperative so you guys can probably handle him."

The way they laughed seem childish and insulting. The new detectives walked up and we went through another set of introductions. I was vaguely familiar with Detective Vince Siragusa who was a couple of years older than me, and I had played basketball against him when I was a sophomore at Fenwick and he was a senior at St. Ignatius. He was a good-natured guy but a little gruff. His partner was a tall athletic looking woman named Becky Rice. They quickly took control of the scene without insulting anybody and then came back to me. I finished up my interview with the professional acting detectives and was more than ready to head home.

Chapter 3

Waking up on Friday morning, I was still bothered by some of the things that I had witnessed and heard on Thursday. I was also a little hung over and disappointed after ending the previous evening with a stop at the green mill on the way home and having a couple of more beers. Gus Kezios was behind the bar and informed me that my friend, Emma Merlin, had not been there in a while and had told Gus that she was going to Arizona to learn how to do some kind of desert sculpture.

My usual morning run was just the thing to sweat the booze out of me, and the cold shower afterward jolted me back into focus. We were busy at the station as usual, and Elaina and I needed to jump on our most recent case, the murder of Cheryl Greenberg. We also had to work overtime the next couple of days since we had both put in to have Sunday off to attend my dad's annual day before Labor Day barbecue.

The continuing hot humid weather wasn't affecting my appetite, and I had the ingredients for one of my favorite breakfasts of French toast, scrambled eggs and lots of bacon. The bacon got started first then eggs were cracked into two different bowls. The scrambled eggs got a splash of whole milk and a couple of shakes of hot sauce, while the eggs for French toast also got a splash of milk and a healthy dose of pure vanilla extract.

When the bacon was finished, I placed the five slices on a paper towel and then poured in the scrambled eggs. Three slices of brioche bread were soaked in the egg batter and placed on a flat iron griddle previously heated and greased with butter. The scrambled eggs when into a plate with the bacon and the lightly browned French toast went on a separate plate sprinkled with cinnamon and powdered sugar. Then they were drenched in real Vermont Maple Syrup. Nothing goes better with this than chocolate milk for me.

In less than 20 minutes my awesome breakfast was history. The dishes and bowls were rinsed, but the cleanup would have to come later. I donned a cream-colored cotton suit with a short-sleeved white shirt and maroon tie with white stripes. My Beretta was back on my belt with my star, and I was ready to get to work.

At 7:45 AM the traffic on Lakeshore Drive was already heavy and I was glad to have left my up down on the Camaro. The air conditioning was welcome as my dash screen read 92°. It wasn't long before I was pulling into the station parking lot on N. Larrabee St..

Walking into the detectives' room, I spotted my partner Elaina Rodriguez engrossed in something on her computer. She had beaten me to the station as usual. Detective Zileen Baker was also busy at her desk sitting next to her new partner, George Makris who was just starting out in his first assignment as a new detective. All I really knew about him at that point was that he grew up on the Near West Side, attended Whitney M Young High School and graduated from the University of Illinois, Chicago with a degree in criminology after playing baseball for four years on scholarship. He was able to ascend to the detective ranks in about three years as I had, and seemed to be just as eager as I had been..

Everyone in the building appeared to accept him and the fact that he replaced Detective Frank Kozlowski, Zileen's former partner who was on a long term leave after being seriously wounded in action, was a breath of fresh air to many of us who wished Koz well but didn't miss his ultra negative presence. The main thing was that Detective Baker liked him.

I sat down next to my partner, and after finishing something on her screen she looked over at me and asked how things went at 26th and California. Making a long story short, I gave her a quick synopsis of what happened in the courtroom during the Billy Sims trial and my interruption of an attempted carjacking outside of Stella's bar in Ukrainian Village.

"I'll fill in the details later." I said. "I hope your day with the kids was more relaxing."

She smiled and replied "okay, I want to hear more later. Yes. Rosie and Lucy were happy to have me to themselves for a whole day. We stayed in the backyard with the sprinklers on in the morning and then went to lunch at Canton Regio. The rest of the day was too hot to go outside."

A few more detectives began filing in including my good friend Morgan Latner and his partner Henrique Sanchez. They came over to greet us and gave me a few jabs about how I somehow caused a riot at the Sims trial. There is no doubt that all news travels fast in police world. I told him that they had it all wrong and that I had single-handedly taken down Sims and controlled an angry mob at the same time. They seemed to enjoy my BS, and we all had a laugh and went about our work.

My desk phone buzzed, and it was Lieut. Tyrone Whitehead who told me to get to his office with Rodriguez ASAP. I let Elaina know, and she wrapped up what she was doing, and off we went.

The lieutenant's door was open, but I knocked anyway and after looking up from whatever he was doing, he waved us in. He asked me to close the door and motioned for us to sit down.

"As you guys know, we have an ongoing epidemic of carjackings happening every day in this city." He said sternly." The mayor and the brass want this to be the top priority. Any case that is or could be a carjacking in our district will be referenced to the carjacking task force. Each of the six police force areas of the city will have a task force command center. Ours will be at the detective station on W. Belmont Ave. In fact, there will be two detectives from their group coming to talk to you two this morning about your Cheryl Greenberg case. They think it may have been a carjacking gone bad. So expect a visit from Detectives O'Brien and Nijinsky. Any questions?"

We both shook our heads. "No" I answered. "We will be happy to work with them."

"Okay that's all." Whitehead Barked. "Keep me informed. Now get back to work!"

We went back to our desks and worked on several of our cases, returning phone calls and following up on leads and tips, until word came that there were a couple of detectives at the front desk asking for us.

I went down to meet them, and Elaina went into one of the small meeting rooms on the second floor. Downstairs, I immediately spotted two detectives at the front desk.

Approaching them I saw a short stocky guy in his mid-30s with the a short blonde military cut who introduced himself as Detective Roger O'Brien and a tall wiry fortyish guy with shaggy brown hair named Carl Nijinsky. They both wore dark gray suits and seemed equally intense.

After the introductions I led them upstairs to the meeting room where they greeted Elaina and we all sat down at the middle rectangular table. Then Detective O'Brien took the lead and got right to the point. He explained that he and Detective Nijinsky were full-time with the carjacking task force assigned to Area 3 and one of the several detective teams looking into assaults, robberies and homicides that have not officially been classified as carjackings, but that could be crimes committed during failed attempts at auto thefts.

"We think one of your recent homicides, the Cheryl Greenberg case, might fit into that category." O'Brien said." What can you tell us about it?"

Elaina spoke first. We have just caught the case, but we know that she was about to get into her car which is a newer model Lexis which was parked on the street outside a restaurant and Streeterville. It is also not far from her apartment. A witness described her attacker as a middle-aged white male wearing a dark colored baseball cap, gray or blue T-shirt and jeans."

"The witness was 1/2 a block away, when the interaction started" I noted. "He was walking toward them and could tell that Cheryl Greenberg and the assailant exchanged words before Greenberg tossed her purse into the car and started to climb in. The guy grabbed her arm and pulled her fully back out of the car forcefully. More words were exchanged but our witness couldn't tell what was said. They struggled and as the witness got closer to them, the attacker spotted him. He then pulled the gun out of his belt and shot Cheryl Greenberg once in the head before dashing back across the street and running away from the witness and then disappearing into an alley.

Elaina continued. "We will be looking into a possible mugging or carjacking, romantic relationships as well as irate victims or clients. She apparently was one of the top defense attorneys in the city. Nothing is off the table at this point."

Detective O'Brien had listened intently and then spoke deliberately. "We have had several jacking's in your area and some other nearby neighborhoods such as Old Town, Ukrainian Village and Wicker Park, where the perpetrators were described as middle-aged white men or young black kids that seem to be working with white guys in getaway cars. We think your case might be one of those.

"Okay. We will definitely keep that in mind as we look further into the case." I said. "It is interesting that you raised the idea of young black kids jacking cars in concert with older white guys. I saw something like that yesterday in Ukrainian Village. A young kid attempted to jack a lady on Western Avenue and injured her pretty badly, before I ran him off. He sprinted across the street and jumped into a truck driven by a 30 something white guy. The lady was screaming for help, so I couldn't go after him. But, you may have already heard about it. I gave a statement to two of your guys right after it happened."

They looked at each other quizzically. "No we didn't hear about it." Nijinsky responded." We had a team meeting this morning and it didn't come up. Who did you say you talked to yesterday?"

"Detectives Anderson and Solar" I answered.

This time they looked at each other smiling and shaking their heads. "I'm not surprised, Detective O'Brien said with a chuckle. Those two guys are a little different. If you know what I mean."

"No. Not really." I responded.

"Well let's just say that Oscar and Jorge kind of play by their own rules. They don't like to share. They don't even try to work with the rest of the team."

"Yeah, I heard that about them from District 3 detectives that showed up after they left. I'll say one thing for them though. They couldn't have responded any faster, if they had been waiting around the corner. I had given a full statement to Anderson and Solar but the detectives from District 3 still needed one from me. They apologized but apparently even though Anderson and Solar were regularly beating the local detectives to the scene of carjackings, they didn't seem to consider themselves to be part of the same team. They were never interested in sharing evidence. They just wanted all the credit. Personally, I am more than happy to let them have it." I said.

With that, O'Brien and Nijinsky stood up and walked out of the room without saying a word. "Nice to meet you too", I said, as Elaina and I gave each other the what the hell was that look.

Chapter 4

"Well, the carjacking task force must be an interesting group", I said sarcastically.

"Yeah" Elaina agreed. "I can't wait to meet the rest of them."

We didn't have time to dwell on other detectives' cases. We needed to get on top of the Cheryl Greenberg murder while it was still fresh. It was Friday and a holiday weekend, but we figured that the law office of Giordano, Greenberg and Collins would be business as usual.

When we arrived at 33 N. Dearborn St., we checked in at the lobby desk and the guard informed us that the firm was on the 11th floor and was indeed open for business.

As the elevator doors opened, we stepped out and were directly in front of the entrance to the spacious reception area of Cheryl Greenberg's law office, one of Chicago's most prominent criminal defense firms.

A very stern looking woman of around 45 years with short dark brown hair and piercing brown eyes sat behind what seemed to be an unnecessarily large desk. She asked how she could help us rather dismissively, as if she really meant that she didn't think the likes of us could even afford their retainer.

I showed her my ID which seemed to impress her even less. Elaina and I were used to how the relationship between cops and defense lawyers could be strained at times, but for the most part we treated each other professionally. Both sides realized that we played our part in the same game. As my dad has often said to me that I did a service to the community by keeping people and property safe and the defense attorneys made sure that the citizens cannot just be charged without sufficient evidence. Not a perfect system by any means, but the best in the world according to dad.

I asked our frosty receptionist whether Mr. Giordano or Mr. Collins were available. She motioned for us to sit down and we moved to a comfortable waiting area furnished with dark leather chairs and a couch. She got on her phone and spoke for a minute in hushed tones.

"Mr. Collins will be out after finishing a phone call." She said with a smirk on her face that seemed to say she hoped it would be an hour.

Much to her chagrin, I supposed, within a few minutes a young, well dressed slender guy walked briskly into the reception area and introduced himself as Jimmy Collins. He explained that his partner, Matt Giordano, was in trial at 26th and California and would be tied up for at least another week.

Attorney Collins invited us to join him in his office and we followed him down a long hallway which led to seven offices and the conference room. Collin's office was second to last on the left side across from the conference room which was occupied by several people in business suits. It was a fairly large space with a couple of comfortable leather chairs placed in front of his dark hardwood desk. The desktop easily had space for a computer, phone, lamp and a stack of color-coded files.

After we introduced ourselves, Collins spoke first. "I expect you guys are here about Cheryl."

"We are", Elaina and I replied in unison. We all laughed and I let Elaina have the floor. "First of all I want to say that we are very sorry for your loss." Collins nodded. "We know that this is a difficult time for you, but we need to get on this right away, as you well know."

"I totally do." Collins said. "Matt and I discussed this yesterday, and we expected to hear from you today. We both agree that we want to help you in every way we can to find the bastard   that did this to Cheryl."

"Can you tell us whether Ms. Greenberg has had any unusually contentious cases recently?" I inquired.

Collins chuckled and responded. "Well, we have nothing but contentious cases, but I know what you mean. You have to understand that we are a very successful practice and handle many high-profile cases. Our success rate at trial is as good or better than any other firm in the city. But, don't get me wrong. We do lose some intense and expensive trials. Those cases inevitably create some resentment from clients and their families.

"Is Ms. Greenberg as successful in her trial work as you and Mr. Giordano?" Elaina asked.

"Let me put it this way. We have or had, three partners and four associate attorneys in this firm. Matt Giordano is the senior partner and I am the junior partner. Cheryl was a rising star in the defense community and had recently won a couple of cases that got a lot of media attention. Cases like that can cause some hard feelings with the State's attorney's office and the cops involved, but it fades quickly since everyone is too busy to dwell on old news. We all just move on'

"I hear that" I responded. "Still do you know whether Ms Greenberg or anyone else ever received any threats during the last few months?"

At that attorney Collin's facial expression changed dramatically. His brow furrowed, and his smile faded into tightened lips. "As I mentioned earlier, we are in an intense business. It can get very personal. We are used to fielding complaints and even threats occasionally, but lately we have received some calls and emails containing extremely violent and graphic threats. They stand out not only because of their viciousness, but also in that they aren't coming from disgruntled clients or their friends. They are coming from people using racist and misogynistic terms and threatening to rid the Country of basically everybody except Christian white people. We didn't really take the threats seriously until Cheryl was murdered two days ago."

"Do you record your incoming phone calls?" Elaina asked.

"We do." Collins answered. "I will make sure they get to you along with the relevant emails."

"That would be great Mr. Collins." I exclaimed.

"Please call me Jimmy." Collins replied.

"Okay Jimmy, did Cheryl Greenberg have a husband or partner living with her?"

"No", Jimmy answered. "She was single and didn't have kids. Married to her work you might say. We all work long hours around here, but she was off the charts. I used to kid her about not needing an apartment. She often slept on her couch here."

"How about family in the area?"

"She has family in Glencoe and Evanston,"Collins said." There will be a ceremony for close friends and family tomorrow at the Baha'i Temple in Wilmette at 10 AM. I think it would be fine for you guys to attend. It would save you a lot of legwork since many of the people you would want to interview will be there."

Elaina and I looked at each other and nodded. "We just may take you up on that." I said." Thank you for your time. We'll see you tomorrow."

We all stood and shook hands before Collins walked us out to the elevators. "It was a pleasure meeting you." Elaina said.

"And we especially enjoyed meeting your charming receptionist." I added .

Jimmy laughed and replied, "oh yeah, Janice is a real sweetheart. If it makes you feel any better, she treats us the same way."

The elevator doors opened and Elaina and I stepped in and she punched the L.

Back on Dearborn Street, I suggested that we take a quick trip to the Medical Examiner's Office to see if the autopsy report on Cheryl Greenberg was ready and then try to track down our witness. Elaina agreed. At the car she took her usual place in the driver's seat. Our arrangement always reminded me of former partner Vernon Johnson who often extolled the advantages of keeping your eyes on the street. He was wise in many ways.

We made it to the ME's Office on W. Harrison St. in about 10 minutes and after seeing no spots open on the street, Elaina pulled into the gated parking and punched in the code and the gate lifted. We entered the aesthetically challenged concrete and glass structure and went to the security desk where I greeted officer Gladys Reese who was a veteran there and remarkably seemed to remember everybody by name. I introduced Elaina and asked if Dr. Lacey Gorman was working.

Gladys his eyes lit up when she answered. "Child you haven't heard the news? The doctor got a big promotion last month. She's in charge of the whole staff here now."

"Wow! That's great Gladys. Where can I find her now?"

"She's in the main office honey. Just down the hall room 101."

"Thanks Gladys. Good to see you."

"You take care of yourself out there Jack. Nice to meet you, Elaina. You watch out for that child."

"I'll try Gladys. It's a challenge." Elaina responded with a laugh.

We took the short walk down the hall and into the main office. There were several people at the reception desk and a young guy looked up and greeted us. I asked for Dr. Gorman and requested that he tell her that Detective Fallon was here to see her.

In less than a minute an athletic middle-aged woman with shoulder length salt-and-pepper hair fairly bounced into the reception area. She greeted us warmly and asked us to step into her new office. I had known her since before I even became a detective, and Elaina had met her recently through some of our other cases.

Her office wasn't fancy with a view, but it was comfortable and roomy. "Well I see that congratulations are in order Dr. I'm surprised that I didn't hear about this."

"Well we keep a low profile around here. And please you two call me Lacey. I am more of a business administrator now. It is a very different job. Not easier, but the work is very different. But you guys are here on the job. How can I help you? "

"We are working the Cheryl Greenberg case." I answered. "You got her here a couple of days ago so we're hoping the autopsy report is finished."

Dr. Gorman punched in a few things on her computer and looked at her screen for a minute. "Oh yes. Here it is. Dr. Horowitz sent it in just a few minutes ago. I just need to review it and sign off on it, and it will go to you guys as the listed lead detectives. But I can give you the basics. "

"That would be great!" I exclaimed.

"Ms. Greenberg was shot once in the head with a 22, probably a pistol, and it was a clean temple shot. We have the bullet, and it will be documented and sent over to the CSI team at your station. There were no drugs or alcohol in her system and not much food. It seems she hadn't eaten in at least 10 hours. The only thing in her system was coffee. She wasn't a smoker but, she really liked her caffeine. So, cause of death is the gunshot. Manner of death is homicide."

"Thanks Dr., I mean Lacey. Old habits." I said with a laugh "Good to see you as always and congrats again."

"Good to see you guys too. Come by anytime."

Walking out into the shadeless parking lot the hot humid air was oppressive after the AC atmosphere inside ME's Office. Summer may be coming to an end but you'd never know it. Labor Day weekend in Chicago is often brutally hot and this one was shaping up that way.

Once in the Impala we left the doors open and cranked up the air conditioning until it was safe to close them and let the AC work its magic. We sat in the lot for a few minutes to discuss what we knew so far about our victim.

Elaina began "I don't think this was a carjacking. For one thing most of them don't result in homicides or even any kind of shooting. But, mainly it is the 22 caliber temple shot. That seems more like a planed hit than a random robbery or jacking. To me the questions are why and who."

"I'm not really completely ready to rule out an attempted jacking, but there are definitely some things about it that bother me. The attempted carjacking that I saw yesterday was similar in that the perp approached a woman on the street just as she was getting into her car. Some words were exchanged, and she resisted. The difference is that the kid grabbed her violently and threw her to the ground. He was about to get into her car, when I chased him off. He was young, but he wasn't afraid. He only ran, after his ride signaled him."

"Did you say that the driver was an older white guy?" Elaina asked. "Yeah. I'd say he was in his late 30s or early 40s. They struck me as an unlikely pair. The kid never displayed a gun, and I didn't see one in the truck, but that doesn't mean there wasn't one. You also have a good point about the clean shot to the head. It's more indicative of a straight up murder. Let's see if we can track down our witness. What was his name again?"

"Jay Farrell ." Elaina responded. "He lives on E. Huron St. in Streeterville."

"Okay", I said. "Let's go meet with old Jay."

Chapter 5

While Elaina drove us toward E. Huron St., I used my handy handheld computer and tapped into our database and found the initial statement given by 40-year-old Jay Farrell. There was nothing in the statement that we didn't already know, other than Mr. Farrell works remotely as an IT consultant. This was good news since we figured that we should be able to find him at home.

We pulled up in front of Farrell's high-rise apartment building and we entered the front doorway announcing ourselves to the doorman sitting at his desk near the entrance. The round faced older gentleman pleasantly greeted us and asked how he could help. Turned out he was a retired Chicago cop and was more than ready to help. He reminded me of my uncle Don.

The helpful old guy, named Richie, said that he had been working his shift since 7 AM and that he hadn't seen Mr. Farrell all day. I asked him what he knew about our witness, and he said that Jay Farrell seemed like a good guy. He had a few friends. They would come by occasionally, but he lived a fairly simple life. He generally went out once or twice a day to do some shopping or take a walk.

Elaina asked our newfound friend Richie Cook to call up to Mr. Farrell's apartment for us. He gladly obliged, and after several attempts he seemed puzzled. "That's odd" he said. "Jay usually answers right away. He has a 1 bedroom. It isn't very big."

"Does Farrell keep his car in your parking area?" I asked.

"Yeah, he has a spot. Let me look it up." Cook pulled up a screen with a list of tenants and their assigned parking spaces with their vehicle and license plate information. Jay Farrell had parking space 317 and owned a white Honda Accord with Illinois plates.

The doorman then swiveled his chair so that he was looking directly at one of the three close circuit monitors. He had the keyboard, and up popped level 3 of their parking garage. He was able to scan the lot and got to parking space 317.

To our surprise there was a tall slim man with sunglasses and a dark baseball cap approaching the Honda. He reached for the driver side door, and it opened right up for him. He got in and started it.

"Is that Jay Farrell?" I demanded.

"Hell no!" answered the doorman.

"Elaina we need to go now!"

She understood immediately. We rushed out to our car. As we got in, we spotted the white Honda pulling out of the parking garage exit and turning the wrong way on this one-way street heading West. We needed to pull a U-turn to follow him. I put the blue light on the dash and hit the siren. We were now in full pursuit.

I called in our location and a description of the white Honda and the license plate. I also called for units to go to Jay Farrell's residence and make an emergency wellness check. Elaina was an excellent driver, and she needed all of her agility and skills to maneuver through the unsuspecting oncoming traffic.

Whoever was driving the Honda showed total disregard for everyone else on the street and his own safety. When he got to Michigan Avenue he drove right into moving traffic and turned right heading North. We followed as some of the traffic slowed or stopped upon hearing our siren. The Honda swerved across two lanes and turned left on Chicago Avenue going west narrowly avoiding a southbound CTA bus. The bus slowed and stopped but was left with its butt end blocking part of the street. Elaina pulled around just missing a couple of SUVs that had pulled over and continued after our suspect who was now about 1/2 a block ahead of us.

The radio was crackling with patrol officers announcing that they had joined the pursuit and the dispatcher letting us know that an all- points bulletin had been put out on the white Honda, and that officers were already at Farrell's apartment building.

Our maniacal suspect wasn't slowing down and was still throwing caution to the wind. A squad car pulled up behind us and we heard on the radio that another car was a couple of blocks ahead of us on Chicago Avenue. We kept on busting through one intersection after the next each with its own hair-raising experience.

Passing through the West Town neighborhood we all ran an obstacle course avoiding a work van and a kid on a bike who had earbuds on and had no idea we were coming. It was a miracle he wasn't killed, although he had to jump the curb to avoid the Honda causing the bike to flip and entangling the kid in it on the sidewalk.

Then right in front of the Beatniks restaurant just past Ashland Avenue the white Honda hit a pothole causing the driver to swerve to the right hitting a dark blue Ford at the driver side door. His car bounced off after causing a major dent and took off with us on his tail.

After several more blocks of dangerous pursuit, I noticed a squad car blocking the traffic heading west. Lights were flashing, and the siren was wailing. Some traffic was still coming at us going east. The driver we were chasing didn't slow down at all. I thought he was going too fast to avoid a life-threatening collision. At the last second, he swerved the Honda around the patrol car clipping a gold Toyota Camry's back bumper knocking it off and then hit the gas.

We needed to slam on the brakes to avoid hitting our sitting duck officers in their car. We carefully pulled around them and could see the white Honda swerving in and out of oncoming traffic about a block ahead of us. We tried to catch up, but our adherence to common sense caused us to lose ground.

We lost sight of them and by the time we got to Western Avenue, we had no clue which way he had gone. We took a guess and turned right toward Ukrainian Village but there was no sign of him. None of the patrol cars in the area reported seeing him either. Damn! The bastard got away.

Just then the dispatcher's voice sent us in a different direction. She informed us that officers had entered Mr. Farrell's apartment and found him face down on his living room floor with a single bullet wound to the back of his head. He was already deceased when they got there.

Elaina did a quick U-turn and I hit the lights and siren again as we sped eastward on Chicago Avenue on our way back to the apartment building on E. Huron St.

The scene at Jay Farrell's apartment building was frenetic. There were uniformed officers outside shooing people away from the entrance, and there were patrol cars there at the end of the block limiting the traffic to official vehicles only. We were waved through and parked near the front entrance. Inside we found doorman Richie Cook standing near his desk speaking to a uniformed officer named Sam Blevins. I knew Sam patted him on the back and told him that Detective Rodriguez and I would take it from there. I told him to stay by the entrance and make sure nobody without a star got in.

Our doorman's round face was flushed, and he was clearly upset. Elaina put her hand on his arm and gently directed him into his chair behind the desk. She assured him that everything was going to be all right and that we needed him to breathe and relax. We were going to need his help.

"Richie, what time did you start your shift today?" I asked.

"I came in at 6:45 this morning. My shift begins at 7:00. I relieved Chester. He said that it had been a quiet night. You know. Nothing unusual."

"How about your day? Anything stand out? Before all of this, of course. "

"No, nothing I can think of. There were a few food deliveries, but that is normal."

"Do you let them up into the building? I inquired.

"No never." Cook replied. They drop the food here and the residents come down to get it. There wasn't anything for Mr. Farrell today."

"Do you take a break for lunch?"

"Not usually and definitely not today. I bring a sandwich or have something delivered. I never leave the building."

"What about bathroom breaks?" Elaina wanted to know.

"Sure I take a few bathroom breaks during the day. I use the men's room right down the hall . In fact, I had a little stomach trouble this morning and stayed in a little longer than usual."

"What time was that?" Elaina followed up.

"Well it must've been around 11:30. I may have been in there for about 10 minutes."

"Okay" I interjected. "We need to go up to Farrell's apartment for a little while. Can you queue up the CCTV footage of the entrance here and of the 11th floor for us while were up there."

"You bet, detectives. I'm happy to help."

Elaina and I went to the elevator, and the door opened immediately. She hit floor 11 and up we went. On Farrell's floor we encountered a couple of uniformed officers and two EMTs exiting his apartment. One of them confirmed that the subject was deceased, and that they had notified the Medical Examiner's Office. Once inside the apartment we saw Jay Farrell face down on the hardwood floor with a large pool of blood around his head. The entrance wound was visible behind his left ear indicating that the shooter was probably left-handed.

There weren't any overt signs of a struggle other than a few magazines strewn around the floor near our victim. We thought that Farrell may have knocked them off the coffee table, when he fell after taking the shot to the head.

At that time the crime scene team arrived and we gave them a quick rundown of what we knew, and we informed the supervising officer Jennifer Kim to send the forensic report to us, and I handed her my card. Just then I noticed a couple of familiar faces standing behind officer Kim. It was Detectives Oscar Anderson and Jorge Solar.

I introduced them to Elaina and asked, "What brings you guys over here?"

Detective Anderson explained that they heard about the bolo on our white Honda, and that it sounded like a possible carjacking from this address. "We're just checking it out."

"Well I'm not sure this case is one of yours, detectives. The victims car was stolen, but that came after the murder took place up here. Seems like a stretch to call this a jacking."

"Okay Detective Fallon. We can see that you have the situation well in hand. We will get out of your way and let you get to it. Nice to meet you Detective Rodriguez." Anderson said. "And please send us a copy of the crime scene report. He and Detective Solar who never said a word walked out to the elevators.

"Are you feeling like I'm feeling?" Elaine asked.

"Yeah. They give me the creeps too."

Chapter 6

The service for Cheryl Greenberg was set for 9:30 AM, so Elaina and I agreed to meet at the station at 8:30 the next day. I woke up Saturday morning to a spectacular sunrise of bright orange and pastel blue colors in the eastern sky. It was going to be another scorcher with possible storms later in the day.

I went for a short run and still came home soaked with sweat. My shower was entirely a cold one, and it got me ready to go. The heat and humidity took the edge off my appetite, so I settled on some orange juice and Frosted Flakes.

The traffic on Lakeshore Drive was already getting heavy, and the lakefront was buzzing on this Saturday morning on the last big summer weekend in the great city of Chicago. I pulled into the lot on N. Larrabee St. at 8:05 and had arrived ahead of Elaina for the first time in a while. The lightweight black cotton suit, I was wearing, felt like I was overdressed just walking in from the car.

Inside the detectives' room Zileen Baker and her new partner George Makris were at their desks and had their jackets off. I followed their lead and hung mine on the back of my chair. My short-sleeved charcoal gray shirt now felt right. The preliminary CSI report from Jay Farrell's apartment was in my email and I was anxious to read it.

Unfortunately, the report didn't contain much that was very helpful at that point. Various blood samples were taken as was material from under Farrell's fingernails for DNA identification. But the results wouldn't be available until the final report. There were multiple unknown fingerprints, and they did not find any shell casings or other evidence pointing to the perpetrator.

The closed-circuit video showed that the perpetrator slipped into the building, while doorman Richie Cook was in the bathroom taking care of his stomach problems. The pictures weren't clear enough for a good identification, but it was good enough to see that it was the same guy that was caught on camera stealing Jay Farrell's Honda.

Elaina came in at about 8:20 looking nice in a dark gray pants suit and a black blouse. I gave her a quick synopsis of the crime scene report, and she said that she would check it out later. "Maybe we will get lucky on the fingerprints or the DNA. Anyway, we know that we are looking for the same tall white guy with the baseball cap."

We didn't have time to get started on any of our other cases, so we decided to just head up to the Baha'i Temple in Wilmette. We dropped by Lieut. Whitehead's office on the way out, but he wasn't in yet. We signed out a car for the day and Elaina took the key fob for a white Chevy Impala.

When we climbed in to our car, we left the doors open for a minute, cranked up the AC and were grateful for the white Impala with cream colored cloth seats. We closed the doors and Elaina turned to me and said, "Okay Jack. Where the hell is this place?"

"Oh, it's directly north along the lake. Take Lakeshore Drive all the way and then just follow Sheridan Road up to Wilmette. When we get to it you can't miss it. Have you ever been up that way?"

"No. I never had any reason to. I hear it's pretty fancy up there. Do you know the place?"

"Not really. I drove past it one time when my sister and I went to Gilson Park which is a beautiful place on Lake Michigan right across the street from the Baha'i Temple. Molly doesn't live too far from the park in the Northwestern University area."

"Okay. Cool." Elaina said. "Lead the way."

With the Impala fully cooled down, the ride up the Lakeshore Drive past Lincoln Park, Uptown and the Edgewater neighborhood was pleasant and gave us some time to catch up in a way that we usually don't at work. Elaina informed me that the renovation of her home in Pilsen was finally completed, after the bombing there in April had devastated the porch and front end of their house.

She also related that her little girls Rosie and Lucy and husband Paco were all doing great, and they all would be at my dad's barbecue the next day. They were bringing homemade salsa, guacamole and tortilla chips.

Leaving the Drive, we continued on Sheridan Road through the North end of Edgewater then past Loyola University and Rogers Park before entering Evanston and driving past some stately homes and the nearby parks and beaches along Lake Michigan before continuing past Northwestern University's Ivy League type campus and then coming to the Wilmette Yacht Club on the right and the grand domed Baha'i Temple on the left. We turned left and found the parking lot nestled on the green manicured property surrounding the temple. Elaina looked at me and with eyes wide open simply said, "Wow!"

The amazing structure sat in the middle of swaths of green grass, trees, gardens and small pools with fountains. The ornate structure stood alone and its towering dome seemed to reach toward the blue cloudless sky. We found a parking spot, and joined a number of other darkly clad people walking silently toward the temple.

Once inside, we picked up pamphlets being handed out concerning the service for Cheryl Greenberg and one explaining the history and purpose of the Baha'i Temple and philosophy. The service included several musical pieces performed by a trio featuring a cello, guitar and flute. The other pamphlets described the unusual construction process which began in 1912 and was completed in 1953. It was the second of eight Baha'i temples built all around the world and was meant to serve all of North America. Their philosophy is one of unifying all the world's religions, and the temple is open to the public as a devotional space for people of any faith.

We chose seats in the back of what was seating for approximately 300 people, so that we had a good view of everyone that attended the service. About half of the seats were already filled and more people kept streaming in. I noticed Jimmy Collins sitting on our side of the gallery near the front next to a silver haired gentleman in an expensive looking black suit.

To our left I could see some familiar faces from the State's Attorney's Office including Terrance Goggins and Paige Owira. They were sitting in the same section, but not in the same row or very near each other. I also recognized a few attorneys from the Public Defender's Office that worked with my dad. I figured that he would have been there if he wasn't engulfed in trial and preparing for his annual labor day weekend barbecue

Soon the service began with some sweet and sorrowful music from the trio set up in front of the crowd and next to a podium. The music softly faded into the warm air. There was some air conditioning, but it was no match for the humid air and the 138 feet high domed ceilings and wide open space that can seat as many as 1200 people. The approximately a dozen fans placed around the spacious hall probably helped, but it was difficult to tell. A tall stately looking man wearing a black suit and a multicolored Star of David yalmulke rose from his seat and walked to the podium.

The man introduced himself as Rabbi Shimon Goodman of the North Shore Congregation Israel. He told the gathering the story of how he had known the Greenberg's for nearly 30 years, and how he had watched them all grow individually and as a family. He recalled Cheryl as a bright energetic child who was driven to excel at whatever she did such as playing the piano and swimming at New Trier High School. He followed her during her college years at Colorado College and then Northwestern Law school. And, he had always admired her thirst for knowledge and meaning and her willingness to accept and embrace others regardless of who they were.

Elaina leaned over to me and whispered, "We sure could use more of that couldn't we Jack."

As I nodded in agreement with her idea, I noticed a tall slender man somewhere in his late 30s dressed in a gray suit coat, a white shirt without a tie and black pants stand up and start easing himself past others seated in the last row across the aisle from us. I nudged Elaina and she glanced over at the guy who was also wearing aviator style sunglasses. Something about him looked familiar.

"I'm going to see where that guy is going. Don't get up. It may not be anything." Elaina responded, "Ok. I'll be here."

I stood up and edged past Elaina and headed for the entrance, where the tall guy had disappeared into a few seconds earlier. The hallway was wide and extensive since it curved around the entire circumference of the structure. So, I decided to quickly check out the nearest men's room. He wasn't in there so I hurried to the doors to the outside and went out into the heat immediately realizing that the temple was not really that hot after all. I spotted my guy out in the parking area. He was moving so fast he was almost running. He kept looking back to see if anyone was following him, until he got to a silver Ford F150 truck, jumped in and then sped out of the parking lot and turned right. He was quickly out of sight.

I was tempted to go after him or call it in, but there was no basis for it. So, I decided to go back to the service. Inside, I could see that Rabbi Goodman had finished up, and a young woman was telling some stories about Cheryl that had the gallery laughing. Elaina whispered, "that is Cheryl's sister Jill." She asked about the guy and I said that I wasn't sure, and that he drove away in a silver truck.

At the end of the ceremony we all were invited to gather at the home of Cheryl Greenberg's parents home on Park Ave. in Glencoe immediately following the service. Everyone exited the temple listening to more soothing music amid the good vibes of a life's celebration. We stopped near the doors, but to the side. At one point Paige Owira came out and walked over to us. She greeted me and I had to pause before introducing her to Elaina. She looked stunning in her black sleeveless dress. "Nice to see you again Detective Fallon", She said." I would still like to talk to you about the Sims case, but this isn't the right time or place. We won't be going over to the Greenberg's home. Goggins doesn't think it would be a good idea. I don't agree but why fight it? You know."

She smiled and winked at me, and I melted even more. She said goodbye and offered her hand to me and pressed her business card into my palm and kept it there for a while, as she looked hard at me. She then turned and walked away. Elaina looked at me and said, "You can pop your eyes back in your head now Jack. Something going on that I don't know?"

"I'm not really sure." I responded." I'm definitely going to find out though." I looked down at her card, turned it over and saw her cell number and the words, "Please call me." I knew that I certainly would.

We stood by and observed the crowd of several hundred people walk out until near the end, when Jimmy Collins came by with the silver haired sharply dressed man, he had been sitting next to in the third row. Family members followed, but we decided not to approach them there. Elaina and I both felt it would be better to speak to them back at the parent's home.

Attorney Collins greeted us and introduced the other guy as his partner, Matt Giordano. We shook hands all around and Mr. Giordano kind of took over the conversation. As it turns out, he was friendly and informal despite his serious and sophisticated appearance. He thanked us for attending the service and expressed what a devastating loss this had been for Cheryl Greenberg's family and their law firm.

I mentioned to Matt that we felt it would be more appropriate to save our questions of Cheryl's family for the more relaxed environment of her parents home. Giordano agreed and added that he would be more comfortable there too. We all agreed to meet up again at the Greenberg residence on Park Avenue in the quintessential North Shore suburb of Glencoe.

The drive north on Sheridan Road through Wilmette, Kenilworth, Winnetka and into Glencoe was very pleasant once the AC kicked in again. The houses on both sides of the road were varied in architecture and impressive. But the estates and mansions on the lake side were jaw-dropping. The well-manicured lawns and monitored driveways were only interrupted by occasional stretches of leafy parks overlooking the lake and their village beaches.

After slowly navigating a winding hilly stretch of Sheridan road connecting Winnetka to Glencoe the road straightened out, and after about a mile and 1/2 we came upon Glencoe's lakefront park which overlooks Glencoe Beach. The north end of the park is bordered by Park Avenue so when we reached that intersection, we turned left and saw all the cars in front of our house on the right. People were streaming in, so we drove past about 1/2 a block and parked on the street. We walked on the impressive Parkway leading right to Lake Michigan which we could see from the sidewalk. Everyone seemed to be walking around the three-story Frank Lloyd Wright style house. We followed the others through the driveway and around to a medium-sized backyard populated by several mature shade trees and colorful flower beds. Tables and chairs were all around, and a bar and hors d'oeuvres table were set up near an entrance into the sunroom at the back of the house.

I was more than tempted to grab a stiff drink, but one stern look from Elaina snapped me back into focus. We each grabbed a small plate of food and a soft drink and just took it all in for a while. Before long Giordano and Collins came up to us with an older couple and introduce them as Mort and Shirley Greenberg.

We thanked them for the opportunity to attend the lovely service and to come to their home. We explained that unfortunately we had work to do. They were clearly shaken and still in the early stages of grief, but they both managed to be gracious.

Elaina took the lead and directed her question to Mrs. Greenberg, as she looked warmly at her and placed her hand on the wounded mother's arm. I could tell she didn't need to explain that she was a mother too.

"Can you tell us about your daughter's friends?" Elaina asked.

"She had wonderful friends." Shirley Greenberg responded clearly becoming emotional. "They were always welcome here and she has maintained relationships with many of them as you can see around you. "

"Were there some serious romantic relationships?" Elaina followed up.

"She dated some at new Trier and in college, but nothing seemed to click for her. She was always driven to do well in her studies and sports, so she didn't really have a lot of time for dating. I guess that drive continued in her legal work. We didn't see her as much in recent years." She concluded.

I turned my gaze to Mr. Greenberg and asked, "Do you know if Cheryl was getting any threats or mentioned being worried about her safety for any reason?"

Mort Greenberg grabbed my arm and said "Let me get you a drink. Come with me." He led me toward the bar, but stopped short of it and turned to me. "Cheryl shared some things with me that she wouldn't with her mother. For the past six months or so she and the other partners at her firm had been receiving threats, and recently they had been getting more frequent and more violent. Some were directed specifically at her about being Jewish, but mostly the threats were about their representing black and Latino criminals etc. It was all vicious and bigoted."

"Did they report the threats to the Chicago PD or FBI?" I wanted to know.

"Yes. Cheryl said they contacted both, and they recorded many of the calls and saved them, but they weren't sure whether anything was being done about it. Maybe now........" he cut what he was saying short and went to the bar and ordered a vodka and club soda.

I thanked him and walked back to Elaina who was now alone. I guess we both decided that the parents had had enough of our questions for that day. Maybe any day. Elaina said that Mrs. Greenberg had pointed out some of Cheryl's friends. So, we spent the next hour interviewing friends of our victim.

Most of what the friends had to say mirrored what Mrs. Greenberg had already told us. Their knowledge of any threats was minimal and vague. One thing of interest, though, was that during law school at Northwestern Cheryl had come out about being lesbian and had started dating women. As far as they knew there hadn't been anything serious.

At that point Matt Giordano walked up and politely interrupted our last interview with Cheryl's friends. We were pretty much done speaking to the last one, an attractive light brown haired woman named Teresa O'Rourke who excused herself. We then turned our attention to Attorney Giordano.

His mood had turned from somber to steely and serious. "It's time that I lay out some things for you guys but not here." He said in a deep commanding tone. I couldn't help envisioning him in front of a jury making quite an impression.

"What have you got in mind?" I asked as Elaina looked at him intently.

"Let's get out of here and take a little walk to the beach. "Lead on." I answered.

We followed Giordano around the side of the house and down the driveway to the sidewalk. I took my jacket off and held it in my left hand, as we enjoyed a short walk to the Bluffs sitting above the picturesque Glencoe Beach. At the edge was a low stone wall and a few viewing benches providing a panoramic look at the wide beach inhabited on this hot summer day by groups of kids and families laying out on blankets and towels and cooling off in the waters of the great inland ocean called Lake Michigan.

We stopped at the approximately 3 feet high stone wall and moved to the last bench on the far right of the viewing area above the sloping heavily vegetated bluff leading down to the sand. There were a couple of people at the other side of the first bench taking pictures and talking among themselves. "I needed to get us away from everybody before I told you some things." Giordano began. "I hope you guys don't mind."

Elaina and I shrugged and responded with "No. We're fine. No problem. We're listening." I said.

"Okay. Here it is. Cheryl had a client named Victor Kirilenko who was charged with extortion and murder of a business owner in

Jefferson Park on the Northwest Side. The business was very successful in over the road trucking and local delivery services. The owners were also Russians and Kirilenko was putting the squeeze on them for the Russian mob. The FBI had been called in, and they had him on wiretaps threatening the business owners and admitting to murders and other crimes to some of his Russian mob cronies."

"All right. I understand why you wanted some privacy. Is there any connection to Cheryl's murder?"

Giordano responded. "I am not really sure because Kirilenko was murdered a couple of weeks ago in his apartment in Ukrainian Village with a 22 shot to his left temple."

"Whoa!" I exclaimed.

"Yeah but that's not all." Matt continued. "Kirilenko was preparing to flip on a whole shitload of Russian gang members. Cheryl set it all up, and they already had one sit down with the State's Attorney's Ofice and some FBI agents. They were very interested in what he had to say, and Cheryl was pleased with the deal they were talking about. I have all of her files on the case in my car. Frankly, I am worried about my safety and everyone else in my firm. I want to give the files to you today. Nobody knows that I plan to do this. Will you take them?"

I took Elaina by the arm and walked her to the other end of the viewing area. "What you think?" I asked my partner.

She looked at me hard. "I don't know what to think Jack. I've never come across this situation before."

"Me neither." I agreed. "But it could definitely be related to Greenberg's murder. And technically he isn't their client anymore. I'm not sure he should be doing it, but I don't think we are doing anything wrong by accepting evidence. I think we should take the files."

"Oh dios mio!" Elaina let out while crossing herself. "Okay compadre. Here we go!"

At that instant a shot rang out, and a bullet hit the back of the bench that Matt Giordano had just sat down in. I told Elaina to get behind the stone wall, and I ran over to Giordano and grabbed him and took him with me over the wall and ducked behind the heavy stone fortress barrier. We had to take a prone position and hold on to bushes to keep from sliding down the bluff as more shots slammed into the stone wall cracking and splintering slabs of stone

I called 911 and reported that we were under fire at the Glencoe Beach on Park Avenue. We had no chance to look up or fire back. I just hoped that whoever it was wasn't walking up on us as we waited. But we didn't have long to wait. In what seemed like one minute the sound of sirens and slamming doors were upon us.

We could hear running footsteps and voices calling out my name. I pulled myself up by the roots of the bushes and climbed over the wall. Elaina and Matt followed, and we identified ourselves to a group of Glencoe police officers led by the large imposing figure of Capt. Dave Norris. Soon police cars from Winnetka and Highland Park started showing up, and they flooded the neighborhood looking for the shooter. Capt. Norris asked us to meet him at the Glencoe Police Department which turned out to be about five blocks away. Thus, the immediate response. We walked back to our cars with a couple of Glencoe patrol officers, and then followed a patrol car in our vehicles to the Police Department on Hazel Avenue.

We all sat down with Capt. Norris and an investigator to give our statements. After about 1/2 an hour we wrapped it up and headed out to the small parking area on the side of the building, where we accepted three boxes of files from Attorney Matt Giordano and wished him a nice night with a laugh all around.

Our drive back south down Sheridan Rd. and then Lakeshore Drive exposed the same summer scenery as the ride up there had but it seemed completely different. Elaina was more animated than I had seen her in months, and I felt excited and angry. This case was getting me fired up. We were both ready to go. Bring it on!

Chapter 7

Sunday morning, the day before Labor Day, I awoke to a bright golden sun hanging over Lake Michigan beckoning me. My mind needed a reset after Saturday's events on the North Shore. So, I put my swimming suit on with a white T-shirt and running shoes. In two minutes I was out the door and running towards Montrose Beach.

The weather was still warm at 7:00 AM, but not as humid as it had been the last few days. The foot and car traffic were light, so I breezed along on my run. In less than 10 minutes I was in the park nearing the lake. The parking lot was mostly empty, as was the beach. I ran all the way over the sand, until I stopped about 6 feet from the water, where I kicked off my shoes, dropped my T-shirt and sprinted into the cool refreshing water of Lake Michigan.

Early September is actually one of the best times to swim in the lake. I continued out a couple of hundred yards and then just treaded water enjoying the panoramic view of clear blue sky, blue water extending over the horizon, coastlines reaching north and south and the city skyline of Uptown. The dedicated swimmers were already in the water. Some wore wetsuits, but many did not. There were a few kayakers along the coastlines and some sailboats already out in the distance.

What a great way to start a summer day in Chicago. I stayed in for about an hour and it was really mentally and physically refreshing. I swam back to shore and walked through the shallow and stood on the wet sand at the edge of the water for a few minutes letting the warm breeze dry me off and enjoying the view for a little longer.

I put my T-shirt on and picked up my running shoes and walked to the first grassy area and knocked the sand off by feet before donning the Brooks runners and jogging the rest of the way home.

I took a shower with my usual cold blast at the finish. It had the usual effect. I felt awake, alert and ready to face the day. And this day I always look forward to. It was traditionally our biggest family event and my dad's favorite day for family and friends to get together.

I gave him a call, and it was a pleasure to hear his voice sound so happy and healthy. "Top of the morning Jackie boy!" He announced, when he answered his cell phone. "Are you getting ready for Chicago's greatest family barbecue event of the year?"

"I sure am dad," I responded. "I'm planning on bringing a case of Miller High Life. What else can I bring?"

"I think we're pretty well covered Jackie. There are so many people bringing things including your partner Elaina who called and told me about her homemade salsa and guacamole. That sounds awesome. I have enough brats, kielbasa, burgers and chicken for 50 people, and there are others bringing all kinds of salads veggies, chips, cheeses and desserts. I have enough pop, beer and other spirits to make a New Year's Eve party blush."

"How about watermelon dad? Is anybody bringing some of those? They would go great in a day like today."

"Not that I know of," dad responded. "If you really want to, you can do that."

This made me happy. Anything I could do to put my dad's favorite day over the top was great. Especially after my mom died, my brother and sister and I knew that our family traditions had become even more important to our dad ."Okay watermelons and beer coming your way."

Next I called my buddy and fellow detective, Morgan Latner. He and his family were always invited, and I was checking to make sure they were coming. Morgan assured me that he and his girlfriend, Tina, would definitely be there, but his brother Reggie and parents probably wouldn't make it since they were going to try to catch up on some lost time on the lake in their recently repaired boat. I had to laugh along with Morgan since it was because of us that their boat got shot up, when we used it in one of our previous cases.

"Ok." I chuckled. "Don't rub it in." I told him what I was bringing, and he countered that he had some of his mom's famous baked beans and that Tina was bringing sangria. I couldn't help thinking that it was going to be a memorable day.

I checked in with my partner, Elaina, and she and her family were getting ready to go to Sunday Mass and would get to my dad's house around 11:30. My arrival would probably be a little earlier, I informed her. Her kids were calling for her in the background, so she signed off and it left me with some time to relax to some music before heading out to the BBQ.

At 10:30 I got into my Camaro, put the top down and drove out into a gorgeous warm summer day. The sun was bright calling for sunglasses, and the air rushing over me gave me a euphoric feeling. I decided to take Fullerton Avenue west all the way to Gale Wood and before long, I was pulling onto my old Street and into the driveway at my dad's home.

It was early, but there were already several cars parked on the street near the house. It wouldn't be long, before the whole block would be filled with the vehicles of those attending the party. There were never any complaints from the neighbors, partly because the crowd was never unruly, but also because everyone on the block was invited and many attended.

I grabbed the watermelons and walked to the backyard and was immediately rushed by my brother Barry's little boys Rory and Ian. I handed each of them a watermelon and told them to score a touchdown by running over the goal line and handing them off to grandpa. They squealed in delight and my dad opened his arms wide, as the dozen people watching them cheered loudly. The four-year-old Ian handed his watermelon football right over to grandpa but six-year-old Rory had to be stopped from spiking his by his dad, brother Barry. They both pranced around for a while, as the crowd laughed and applauded.

After making the rounds starting with my dad and continuing with several familiar neighbors and ending with uncle Don, I went back to my car and retrieved the case of Miller High Life bottles and found them a home in one of my dad's large ice filled coolers.

My father was in his glory already cooking loads of sausages which would be covered and set aside. The burgers and chicken would be cooked next. He usually started serving food around 12:30 or 1 o'clock, after most of the guests had arrived and had a chance to have a drink or two.

I spotted my uncle Don sitting by himself, and I walked over and sat next to him at one of the picnic tables. He was already enjoying one of my Millers as was his habit. He liked to bring his own Miller Lites but start out with a few of mine. It was a family tradition of sorts.

"How are you doing Jackie boy?" uncle Don roared slapping me on the back. "Are you putting them away faster than your dad can get them off?"

It was a running joke for uncle Don, at least he always thought it was funny. He viewed my dad's work as a defense lawyer as some kind of quasi-criminal endeavor. Everything for him was black and white, and he tended to see most things as being black. This was always amusing to me, because my mom, his sister, also saw everything in black-and-white, but saw most things as being white. My dad, on the other hand, was the master of shades of gray. These philosophical differences that often lead to very interesting and lively discussions later on in the evening at many family get-togethers in the past.

The backyard was filling up with hungry and thirsty partiers, as my sister Molly came by to say hi to me and Uncle Don. She had a glass of white wine in hand and a jovial smile as usual. Her positive nature seemed to be reflective of the group in general. Everyone was there to have a nice time and nobody was disappointed.

My buddy Morgan and his girlfriend Tina made their way through the crowd and joined our table. He knew Molly well and had met Uncle Don a couple of times. My uncle loved all things law enforcement. So, he had taken to Detective Morgan Latner immediately.

"Hey there Morgan." Uncle Don said in greeting. "How did you get such a beautiful lady? "

Tina blushed and smiled. She is a very attractive tall blonde who also played basketball at Evanston High School. She and Morgan didn't date then, but had been together for a few years by that time. She maintained her own apartment in Evanston, but they were together as much as their schedules allowed.

"Come and join us at the law and order table," Uncle Don continued. "Jack, your father has the whole place full of those damn defense lawyers."

Molly cut him off. "Cut it out uncle Don. That's my father you are talking about." She left and put a kiss on my uncle's head that calmed him down and ended that line of conversation.

My dad announced that the sausages were available, and that burgers and chicken would be coming up later. Just then Elaina arrived with her husband Paco and their little girls Rosie and Lucy. The girls immediately joined in with Rory and Ian, and some other kids who were chasing each other around the yard in some kind of improvised game of tag free-for-all.

Elaina greeted my dad Ed and introduced Paco to him and the rest of the Fallon Cogan clan. After getting around to everyone that she knew, she grabbed a glass of sangria and a beer for Paco and joined us. Molly got up to provide more room for Elaina and Paco and announced that she was going to sit with some of those damn defense attorneys. Uncle Don scowled while Morgan and I laughed, and Elaina looked perplexed.

I noticed Molly sit down with some of my dad's fellow public defender attorneys including one named Linda Prassas, an attractive 40-year-old woman with long light brown hair and hazel eyes. She was the attorney who was representing Billy Sims and had cross-examined me. Molly looked back at me as she sat down and winked, and I gave her the finger. We both laughed.

The wonderfully warm September afternoon seemed to fly by. Everyone there appeared to be eating and drinking to their hearts content. I sure did my part having two sausages, a burger, chicken with baked beans, guacamole and tortilla chips and some homemade cookies. I didn't even get to the watermelon, but it went fast anyway. The Millers also went down easily.

After a couple of hours of mingling and moving from table to table, I found myself back sitting with uncle Don, my cousin Claire and Morgan and Tina. Everyone was full of food and feeling no pain. Elaina came by and sat down prompting uncle Don to start telling family stories. He was in his glory.

Eventually he got around to me and my obsession as a little boy with becoming a cop. "That is all little Jackie ever talked about. Oh he loved basketball and football, but it was nothing compared to his passion for catching the bad guys. Whenever he and the other kids played cops and robbers little Jackie was always the cop. He wouldn't even consider changing places. Even older brother Barry couldn't make him be a bad guy, and Lord knows he tried. Jack would rather take a beating than be the bad guy.

Everyone got a kick out of uncle Don's stories and Morgan and Elaina said that they could relate. "I have to admit being a Chicago cop is the only job I have ever wanted. This is where I belong. Where I need to be."

Uncle Don was starting to get a little sentimental. He was a tough guy having had a career in the Marines including combat and for many years after that as a doorman at the Intercontinental Hotel on N. Michigan Ave. But his gruff exterior often melted into warm remembrances at family get-togethers."We are all proud of you Jack. Making detective and all. Especially your dad, you know. I make fun of him being a defense lawyer and everything, but he has a job to do too. He knows how hard your job is Jackie boy. That goes for all of you detectives" waving his arm at Elaina and Morgan.

At that moment the landline in the kitchen rang loud enough for me to hear it above the chatter and soft music. I started to get up to answer it, but my dad saw me and motioned for me to sit back down. He hustled through the back door and the ringing stopped.

Elaina remarked that it was unusual to hear a landline these days, and as Morgan and I nodded in agreement, uncle Don informed us that he still had one. He just didn't fully trust the cell phones. He felt safer having one in his apartment.

At that point my dad stepped out into the backyard and called over to me. "Jack give me a hand in the kitchen." I got right up and followed him back into the house.

I hadn't noticed it at first but once inside I was startled by the grim look on my father's face. The bright look in his eyes and broad smile was replaced by an alarming pallor and a furled brow. "What's wrong.? You look terrible."

"Jack I just received a terribly disturbing phone call. Some guy was spewing all kinds of threats aimed at me and the public defender's office using all kinds of racial and ethnic slurs about the people we represent. I didn't recognize the voice and I have an unlisted number here."

"Dad, I'm so sorry. Has this happened before?"

"It has been happening at the office. We are used to it there. We get threats from some disgruntled clients and their families mostly, but in the last couple of months the threats have increased and are mostly concerning our representation of minorities and have become more graphic and vulgar."

"I wish you had told me sooner dad."

"You have so much on your plate already Jack. And, the calls didn't concern you until now."

"What you mean until now?" I asked.

"There's something else," my dad replied. "The guy mentioned you and your partner and Morgan by name. He seemed to know who was here at the BBQ, and he wants to talk to you. He said that he was going to call back in a couple of minutes."

Ring. Ring. The sound of the landline interrupted our conversation, and I walked my dad away from the phone and picked it up. I waited for the caller to speak.

"Listen close Detective Fallon. You are living very dangerously by associating with the defense lawyer scum headed by your traitor of a father. You have done some good work in putting lowlifes away, but you are ruining all that by hanging out with that beaner partner of yours and your black bastard buddy, Latner."

"You are a warped sick asshole!" I exclaimed forcefully.

"We'll see who the sick ones are, when we rise up and take America back for real Americans", the asshole responded.

"Who's the we you are referring to?", I asked. "I'm sure you hang with a real impressive crowd. Why don't you meet me somewhere. I'd love to continue this conversation face-to-face. Maybe I would like to join your little gang."

"We wouldn't have a colored lover like you. We just get rid of your kind. And, the first patriots brigade isn't so little. You'll find that out. We are everywhere. And, if I want to meet you I could do it right now. Or maybe I'll just snatch your brothers little boys or the wet back brats playing with them." He laughed sardonically and hung up.

I put the phone down and went to the drawer where Elaina, Morgan and I had placed our service weapons. I attached my Beretta and holster to my belt and grabbed a brown paper bag and placed Elaina and Morgan's weapons and holsters inside. "Dad stay in the backyard. Tell your people to stay put for now and get all the kids in the house. Morgan and I need to check out the area. Elaina will stay here."

My dad nodded and didn't ask questions. He trusted my judgment and could tell that I needed to act. Now! Outside, I pulled Elaina and Morgan aside and walked them around the side of the house. I handed them their holstered guns and relayed the gist of my conversation with the asshole. They grasped the situation immediately. Morgan and I would go out to the street and Elaina would stay at the house. She would gather all the kids and herd them into the house to play a game or something. She had the most important job, and she knew it.

Morgan and I walked slowly out to the front of the house. There was no rush. We didn't know where we would be rushing to anyway. We surveyed the scene and didn't notice anything at first. There was no one on the sidewalks. Hell most of the neighborhood was in the backyard. There were so many cars and trucks, nothing stood out until I spotted it.

About 100 feet up the block on the opposite side of the street there was a silver Ford F150 parked in between a white Honda CRV and a black Chevy Blazer. I calmly informed Morgan that I thought I recognized the silver F150 and that we should approach it slowly on both sides of the truck. Latner took the sidewalk, and I approached it in the street on the driver's side of the vehicle that was facing us.

Getting closer it became clear that there were two men in the truck and that the engine was running. At about 10 yards away I realized that I had seen the driver before. He was the same guy from Cheryl Greengerg's service at the Baha'i Temple and possibly the guy from the attempted carjacking outside of Stella's. He was wearing the same aviator sunglasses, and as soon as I got to the truck and cleared the front of it he punched the gas and screeched onto the street blowing past me and missing by only inches.

I was really pissed off but had no justification to fire at them. So, I called it in and asked for a bolo concerning a silver Ford F150 driving erratically around Galewood. Maybe we would get lucky and at least get an ID on the driver. The license plates had been smeared with mud, but were definitely Illinois tags.

"What the hell was that?" Morgan asked. I filled him in on the phone call and my previous interaction with the tall thin driver wearing aviation sunglasses. I was embarrassed and angry to have to tell him and later Elaina about the derogatory racial slurs and especially the threats on her children. I also needed to inform my brother Barry and his wife Tammy about the threats made against their children. I would leave it to my dad to tell his colleagues about the threats made against them.

We walked back to the party and all eyes turned to us. There was no point in ignoring everyone's curiosity. I announced that Morgan and I were checking out a crank call that may have been coming from a couple of guys that were on the street in a Ford F150, and that it had driven away when we approached them. We didn't think that they were still in the area or that they posed any immediate threat.

I went over to uncle Don's table, where he was sitting with his daughter Claire and Elaina's husband Paco. I gave them a general explanation of what was going on leaving out the most distasteful language. The idea of the threats still got my uncle riled up. He was older, but had always been a man of action and he wanted to do something. It took me a couple of minutes, but as soon as I calmed him down, I went into the house.

Elaina was in the living room entertaining all the children with a story about a great American cowboy named Alvarez Kelly. I waited until she finished, and the hero was riding off into the sunset before interrupting in telling the kids to report to their parents. Elaina escorted Rosie and Lucy out to their father and then came back. Barry followed her in, and we had a sort of family team meeting.

I informed everyone about the phone calls beginning with my dad's and then recounting mine basically word for word. I could see the alarm on Barry's face and the anger in Elaina's eyes. My dad started trying to apologize for this mess as he referred to it, but I stopped him. "This isn't your fault dad. These are some sick jagoffs, and we need take them out. It's as simple as that. But we all need to be careful and more vigilant than before. It is unfortunate. But it's real."

We all agreed to keep in touch and Elaina and I would, of course, be back at work together the next morning. Yes, we would be working on Labor Day. So, with the fun having been let out of the party like air out of a balloon, the guests began thanking my dad and saying their goodbyes.

Barry, Molly and I began cleaning up, and Elaina insisted on staying to help. So, before long the backyard was nearly back to normal. Uncle Don stayed and had a couple more of my Millers while Molly calmed him down. I offered to stay the night with my dad, but he wouldn't have it. He wasn't afraid, and he could handle himself.

Elaina was finally convinced that the cleanup was done, and I told her that I planned on coming to the station in the morning around 9:00. She said that she would see me then, and they all piled into Paco's Chevy Tahoe, and they were off.

I said my farewells to the family, Morgan and Tina. I asked them if they would like to join me at the Green Mill for a night cap, but they declined. Morgan wasn't a heavy drinker, and he and Tina were ready to go home. I couldn't blame them.

The drive back to Uptown was slow going but uneventful. I decided to put the Camaro to bed at my apartment building before taking a walk to the Green Mill. I was pretty wound up and knew that I might get a little bit drunk.

At the neighborhood watering hole I found a moderately busy early evening scene and found a seat at the bar. Gus Kezios was on duty and popped a Miller for me and asked "And one?"

"Definitely Gus. It's been one of those days" I looked around hoping to see the familiar lovely face of Emma Merlin. I had no such luck. I guess that was too much to ask. Gus brought two shot glasses and poored some Jack Daniels. We clinked glasses and down they went, and he filled them up again before putting the bottle away.

"What's up Gus?" I asked. "You've never had a drink with me before."

"Nothing's up. You just look like you need a friend today. A bartender knows. Besides before you ask? Emma came by yesterday. She said that she was going to Iowa this time for a while to work on some kind of bronze or iron sculptures. Don't ask me. That's what she said."

We clinked glasses again and I proceeded to wash the bad vibes away with Miller High Life, Jack Daniels and conversation with Gus. By the time it was over, I was very glad that I hadn't driven to the Green Mill.

Chapter 8

Labor Day morning arrived a little later than usual for me with a pounding rain on my windows and a pounding throbbing in my head. I read somewhere that the Danish called it carpenters playing in your head. I thought it was funny then, but not now.

I couldn't imagine eating any breakfast or going for a run, so I settled for two Excedrin and a cool shower. It was dark outside and gloomy in my mind. Despite the enjoyable rave with Gus Kezios at the Green Mill, my attempt at cleansing myself of the depressing encounter with the assholes threatening my family and friends hadn't worked. I was now hung over and depressed. The only thing I could think of that would get me out of this funk was to get to work and start finding a way to take the bastards down.

My choice of a black suit with black short-sleeved button-down shirt and a black tie with purple stripe reflected my mood. Driving down the lakeshore in my black on black Camaro I must've looked like one of the bad guys in a James Bond movie. I just wished that I felt the part. Those guys never seem to feel any pain.

When I walked into the detectives' room at 9:20 AM, Elaina looked up from her computer and laughed. She had obviously taken a very different approach to the day wearing a bright blue blazer with white slacks and a yellow low cut blouse. She looked great. I couldn't help reminding myself that she was married and thinking that she probably hadn't spent the night with Jack Daniels and a well-intentioned but crazy bartender. Even my laughing was painful. Ouch!

"You didn't go straight home last night, did you amigo?" Elaina said with one of those I feel great, and I have no sympathy smiles.

"Very perceptive of you Holmes." I replied trying hard not to inflict more pain on myself by laughing again.

Just then Detective Morgan Latner walked into the room. He took one look at me and started laughing so infectiously that Elaina and I couldn't help laughing too, and we all went at it so hard that none of us could breathe or speak. Every time one of us tried caused the other two of us to laugh even harder, and so it went for several minutes. By the time it stopped, I actually felt a little better. It was a wonderful healing tonic.

"Hey Morgan, I thought you had the day off?" I asked.

"I do buddy."   He responded. "But, after the bullshit that went down last night, I needed to put how I feel into work. Anyway, we are kind of comrades in arms even more than usual now." He said with a laugh. "If one of us goes, we all go!"

Elaina and I laughed again nervously. "Mios amigos" she said, giving herself the sign of the cross. "You two are loco but I am truly happy that you will always have my back!"

Detective Latner wanted to know, what we were working on, and I told him about the Cheryl Greenberg case and our adventurous day on the North Shore Saturday. I pointed to the three boxes full of case files on the now deceased Victor Kirilenko and explained how they might shed light on the murder of attorney Greenberg.

"Awesome!" Morgan exclaimed. "Three boxes and three amigos. Let's get started."

So, we spent the next two hours painstakingly going through every piece of paperwork in every file. It was a very tedious process which included correspondences, motions, disclosures from the State's Attorney's Office, police reports and many pages of Cheryl Greenberg's notes. Luckily her handwriting was remarkably neat and legible.

There were numerous references to possible connections that Kirilenko had with a carjacking gang based in or near Ukrainian Village. The gang was allegedly led by a Ukrainian couple named Ludmila Janco and Vladimir Potemkin. They lived in Ukrainian Village and had a large auto body shop near East Humboldt Park.

One police report made a reference to suspected affiliations with the Russian mob and other unknown fringe criminal groups.

Elaina came across some references in Greenberg's notes to contacts with the FBI Office in Chicago at 2111 W. Roosevelt Rd. In fact, it looked like she had an appointment to meet a Special Agent Tony Wright at the FBI Office the next day, Tuesday morning at 11 AM.

"I think we should keep that appointment." Elaina stated. "Kirilenko was getting ready to testify. It would be good to know more about who the targets were. It seems like there may have been federal as well as state charges involved."

"My box is full of heavy shit." Morgan declared. "Apparently there were dozens of threats made against Kirilenko and Greenberg. Some were concerning cooperating with the Chicago PD and the FBI, but there were even more going after Greenberg for being Jewish and for getting scumbag minorities off the hook, when they should be deported, imprisoned or executed."

"It almost seems like the threats are coming from at least two different sources." I said. "I wonder if they could be connected somehow?"

"Who was the lead detective for Chicago PD in the Kirilenko case?" Elaina asked. "It's not in my box. "

"I have it." I replied." It looks like Detectives Brevin Gilmore and Latisha Sayers. They work out of the Shakespeare Station on N. California. Looks like another stop on our list, partner?"

Elaina nodded in agreement. "I need a break from those files guys, and I'm getting hungry. How about some lunch?"

Morgan and I didn't need to be persuaded. My stomach was coming around and my head, with the help of a couple more Excedrins and several glasses of water, had stopped pounding. The carpenters had thankfully taken the rest of the day off, and I was tempted to do the same. It was Labor Day after all and the weather outside had changed for the better as well.

Elaina wanted to try Mr. Beef on N. Orleans Street in River North.

She said that she had heard about the place since being transferred to the Near North in April. Morgan and I were big fans of the place, so we all piled into Elaina's new Jeep Cherokee and took the short ride to one of Jay Leno's favorite Chicago spots for tasty local treats.

Mr. Beef is in many ways just a classic neighborhood hot dog stand. From the street you first notice the oversized sign bearing its name and the iconic red bottle top Coca-Cola logo hanging over the entrance and sidewalk. Inside, is a standard counter in front of a galley kitchen, menu boards and vintage signs that echo days gone by including a few reminding everybody that cash is king.

Elaina was clearly enjoying the classic dive atmosphere. Morgan and I grew up with places like this. In Evanston, Morgan had Mustard's Last Stand and I had Johnnies Beef in Elmwood Park not far from Galewood.

Morgan went with the Italian beef with Italian sausage on top with giardiniera and sweet peppers. I decided on a large Italian beef with everything on it fully dipped and Elaina chose a regular sized barbecue beef. We ordered various soft drinks and shared orders of fries and onion rings sitting at the dark brown narrow table with bench seating which runs down the center of the joint.

By the time we had devoured our classic Chicago food and watched a parade of locals and visitors come in for the same reason we did, we were ready for a change of scenery. Morgan and I had devised a plan which included going back to our apartments and changing into some boating garb and meeting up at Montrose Harbor to board the Latner family vessel. We tried to talk Elaina into joining us, but she was a firm "No!"

"You guys go ahead. Enjoy what is left of the summer. I want to keep going on the Greenberg files. I also want to have a peaceful home to return to." She said with a laugh. "You single guys just enjoy yourselves. As for me, I would like to stay married for a while longer.

This time we all laughed and got back into Elaina's red Cherokee. Latner took the front since his 6'5" frame included the longer legs, and within an hour we were meeting back up at Montrose Harbor joined by our buddy and fellow detective Ricky Del Signore eager to enjoy a warm Labor Day afternoon on Lake Michigan.

I brought a Coleman cooler filled with ice, Miller High Life and some IPAs with some cans of Coke for Morgan. We all walked down to slip 66 and before long we were cruising South in Morgan's high-powered twin-engine speedboat.

We zipped along the lakefront passing Wrigleyville where the Cubs were playing the Dodgers. We continued past Lincoln Park, North Avenue beach and the Gold Coast before settling in with the crowd outside of Ohio Street Beach that we call the playpen. Morgan brought us up close to a couple of other boats full of people that we knew, and we hung out with them enjoying the sun, water and lively music for a couple of hours until the party started breaking up. Our party partners headed back to their boat slips on the river, Monroe Harbor and other destinations. Morgan turned our boat around and started back towards Montrose but then turned right and we headed out into open water. "Let's stay out for a while fellas." The captain said. "We need to savor this last one."

Ricky and I looked at each other and smiled, clinked bottles of Miller together and let out a loud "Yeah baby!" Latner had stopped drinking an hour before as usual, so he just laughed and steered the boat out toward the blue-green horizon of Lake Michigan.

When we got far enough out that the high rising skyline of the great City of Chicago looked like a miniature replica, we dropped anchor. Morgan shut down the engines, turned off the music and set down with us. We were all on the same wavelength and relaxed enjoying the silent serenity interrupted only by the gentle motion of the water lapping up on the side of the boat.

We hung out together drinking beers and talking about Chicago sports, concerts, and old times the way good friends do. Work issues did not get a mention and the most serious thing we talked about was the Cubs pitching problems. The sun was starting to set in the west placing a gold ribbon around the skyline. Then my phone buzzed. I fully intended to ignore it until I noticed that it was Elaina.

"Hold on partner. Slow it down a little and give me a chance to catch up to you. We have been in total mellow mode out here. It may take a second to take it back to your work state of mind."

"Okay. Okay compadre. Where are you?"

"We are still out on the lake. Just finishing a fantastic day watching the sunset."

"So sorry Jack. I am just so excited. Would you like me to call back later?

"No. No. Go ahead. I'm back. Detective Fallon at your service."

She chuckled and continued her train of thought. "This whole situation with Cheryl Greenberg is more complicated and serious than we thought. Who are you with?"

"I'm with Morgan and Ricky. Why?"

"What I have found out is very disturbing Jack. Attorney Greenberg's notes indicate that Victor Kirilenko was heavily involved with a white supremacist group called the First Patriots and that there is some connection to that group and the Chicago PD and the FBI. Her notes are unclear as to what the connections are. We need to clarify that pronto, and there are other issues that she only makes marginal notes about in the file. Jack we need her computers. Like right now!"

"Oh man. Of course. I get where you're coming from in every way. Just know that I trust these guys with my life. Just like I trust you partner. We need to get a warrant for Greenberg's computer and files tomorrow first thing."

"Okay amigo. "I'm glad you had a chance to enjoy the afternoon. I am headed home now for a little late BBQ with Paco and the kids. You get home and get a good night sleep this time."

"Thanks for holding down the fort for me today. I really needed this. Have a good time and stay safe."

I hung up and turned my eyes to my buddies who were giving me an inquiring look. They weren't only my best friends, they were detectives. So, I told them the gist of what Elaina had just informed me and gave Ricky a rundown on the events of the day before at my dad's BBQ. He got the big picture immediately and was pissed off.

"This is some really serious shit guys. We all take for granted that we are in a dangerous business, but you can't discount direct threats. And we all know that as much as we are dedicated to our brothers in blue, there are some bad guys. You can't help hearing the bigoted comments and racial slurs. I'm not familiar with the First Patriots or whatever they call themselves, but the thought of Chicago cops being associated with groups like that is scary."

"We need to keep this to ourselves, and we need to start noticing and listening for any signs that some of our CPD brothers or sisters have gone rogue. Elaina and I are the leads on the Greenberg case. Nobody should suspect that you two know anything about it. Especially, you Ricky. Obviously, Morgan and I are already on their radar after being threatened directly yesterday."

"I hear you. But don't forget that when you two are threatened, I am threatened. I have your backs." Ricky promised.

"We know Ricky." Morgan responded. "None of us should mention Greenberg's files or computers either. We should keep our eyes and ears open though. It sucks to be suspicious of fellow officers, but we need to be real here. Our lives may depend on it. Let's have one last drink to a great day together. "He popped an IPA and pulled two Millers for me and Ricky.

We raised our bottles to each other and the golden setting sun.

Chapter 9

Tuesday morning arrived in a much different light both in the sky and my outlook. Although still troubled by the threats made to both family and friends, I was determined to focus on my work and to carry on as usual.

I left for my morning run around 6:30 and returned at 7:00 soaking wet and invigorated. A cold shower and hearty breakfast of pancakes, Jimmy Dean sausage links and hazelnut coffee did the trick.

By 7:45 I was dressed for a warm summer day working as a Chicago PD detective, the only job I ever really wanted. I hit the road in my black on black Camaro convertible with the top down. The sun was shining bright, the wind was rushing over me, and the view of Lake Michigan was inspiring.

When I walked into the detectives' room, Elaina was standing by the coffee maker engaged in an animated conversation with detectives Zileen Baker and George Makris. As I approached, Elaina gave me some startling news." Oh Jack. We just got a call that attorney Matt Giordano was found shot to death in his office this morning around 7 AM by one of his associate attorneys. It seems that he had been dead for some time. The office was ransacked, but nothing was taken except Cheryl Greenberg's desktop computer. None of her files were missing, and the firm's safe was untouched.

"Damn!" I exclaimed. "This is likely connected to Greenberg's murder. We should be on this one too."

"Yeah. Lieut. Whitehead wants to see us right away. I guess he thinks we should take the case too. Let's go see him."

Whitehead's office door was open and he was up and pacing around the room. He seemed preoccupied, and didn't even notice us at first. We waited at the entrance before he looked up and waved us in and told us to sit down, while he continued to walk around the office.

"We have a situation brewing here detectives!" Whitehead declared in his booming baritone voice. "For the past couple of months there have been increased reports of threats made to attorneys and judges in the city. And, now we have two of Chicago's most prominent defense lawyers murdered within five days of each other. I want you two to take the lead on attorney Giordano. It is most likely connected to the Greenberg killing"

"We think so too, Lieutenant", Elaina responded. "I didn't have time to tell Detective Fallon that Detectives Anderson and Solar from the carjacking task force are already on the scene. They claim to have been on their way to the office to interview attorneys Giordano and Collins, because they considered the Greenberg case to be a carjacking."

"Well they're homicides and they are your cases. You can cooperate with the jacking task force, but you two are in control. Don't forget that."

Elaina and I were grinning from ear to year as we glided out of Lieut. Tyrone Whitehead's office. We felt gratified to know that we had the confidence of our Lieut. He was such a commanding figure standing 6'6" tall with an athletic 250 pound frame and a booming voice that could stop even the most seasoned detectives in their tracks.

We didn't need to say anything further. Elaina signed out our vehicle for the day, a black Chevy blazer, and within five minutes we were on the scene at 33 N. Dearborn St.The high-rise office building was cordoned off and traffic was being diverted on that block to allow the various emergency vehicles access.

Once inside, we went up to the offices at Giordano, Greenberg and Collins Attorneys at Law and encountered fellow detectives Oscar Anderson and Jorge Solar. They both glanced at us, but kept on opening file drawers and issuing orders to some of the uniformed cops on the scene.

"Okay listen up. All uniforms leave the scene right now and wait downstairs. Don't let anyone up here except the Medical Examiner's Office and the Crime Scene Unit." I exclaimed, leaving no doubt who was in charge.

Detective Anderson started laughing in such a way that was more derisive than friendly and Solar shot me a look that made me brace myself for a fight. As he stepped toward me Anderson put his hand on his shoulder and said something in a whisper and turned to me. "Okay hotshot. We caught this case first so you and your sidekick vamos comprende?"

Now, Elaina's eyes flashed and the tension was palpable. "Not a chance Anderson. I don't know what you two are doing here, but this is not a carjacking. It is a homicide and the homicide unit will handle it. If we happen to run across any carjackings will let you know. Now clear out of here and let us do our jobs. And don't touch anything else. You've done enough damage already."

Detective Solar, a powerfully built man about 5'10" and 220 pounds was staring at us and looked ready to charge like an enraged ball. Once again Detective Anderson, a slender guy around 6 feet tall and 170 pounds but wiry and in his early 40s, turned his back to us and whispered something that stopped the impending charge.

Anderson smiled wryly, "Ok detectives. You can have it. You're pretty cocky Fallon. That attitude could get you in trouble in Chicago. We'll be seeing you two around. Be sure to watch your backs. You never know what could happen out on the street." He stepped around me and then Jorge Solar brushed into me on the way out, and as he did Elaina said something to him in Spanish that didn't sound like "Have a nice day."

With the office now cleared we donned surgical gloves and started looking around. It was obvious that there was nobody there and the desk was clean and had nothing on it except a landline. Elaina and I looked at each other. Where the hell is the computer? Of course, Matt Giordano wasn't there. It wasn't his office. This was Cheryl Greenberg's office, and her desktop computer was missing. And what the hell were Detectives Anderson and Solar doing going through her file drawers. I felt a strong sense of relief that we at least had the files that attorney Giordano thought were important. I also had to wonder if these files had gotten him killed.

We walked down the hall into Matt Giordano's office and saw him sitting in his chair slumped forward onto his desk. His head touched up against his desktop computer. Why was that still here I wondered. He had one shot to his left temple with blood on his shoulder and left arm on the desk where his head landed.

I heard a faint voice from down the hall and motioned to my partner to follow me. We drew our firearms and crept quietly toward the voice. It was clearly coming from the office we had visited a few days earlier. There sitting on the edge of his desk and talking from a cell phone was attorney Jimmy Collins who was so startled when we came in with guns drawn that I thought we were going to have another dead lawyer to deal with.

"Hey, sorry Collins." I declared." We didn't know it was you. They should have cleared everyone out of here.

Collins told whoever he was talking to that he had to go and looked at us starting to regain his composure. "I understand detectives. I came over here this morning from court as soon as I heard the news. Of course, I understand the whole crime scene thing, but they let me in and I wanted to check my office. Unfortunately, there was nothing I could do for Matt.

"Well okay counselor." Elaina said. "Since you are here, was anything taken from your office? "

"No. I can't find anything missing and my computer is password protected. It hasn't been tampered with."

I looked at Elaina and asked Collins to take a walk with us to look at attorneys Giordano and Greenberg's offices and cautioned him not to touch anything. He nodded and followed us to Giordano's office first. He looked around and stated that nothing seemed amiss. "Look in the top left drawer of his desk." Collins suggested.

Elaina pulled it open, and we could all see that it contained a midsized laptop computer. She didn't remove it. Instead she looked at the dead attorney's partner and asked "Is this Matt's laptop?"

Collins answered that it was, and that he preferred using the desktop when in the office, and that he usually kept it in the drawer."

"Okay. Let's take a look at Cheryl Greenberg's office." I said. Once there Jimmy Collins looked around and sighed. "I can't believe they are both gone. I feel like I'm living in a nightmare. Somebody took her desktop, and it looks like they went through her file drawers."

"Yeah, well we know who went through her drawers." Elaina offered. "We don't think they took the desktop. What about Cheryl's laptop?"

Collins didn't hesitate. "She always had it with her. It should be at her apartment I guess."

At that moment the Crime Scene Unit entered the suite of offices followed by the Medical Examiner's Office representatives. We directed them to attorney Giordano and ushered Jimmy Collins out the door with us.

I spotted Sgt. Corbin Maris of the crime scene team getting out of the elevator heading toward us. I knew Maris well and was glad to know that he was on this case. I informed him that Elaina and I had the lead and asked him to direct any reports to us. "Oh check any good prints that you find against Detectives Oscar Anderson and Jorge Solar. Unfortunately, they got in there ahead of us and were handling potential evidence."

"You're shitting me!" Maris erupted." Who are these morons?" His round face turned red and his blue eyes seemed to turn darker. He was a short barrel chested veteran with a military haircut and a stand up straight military posture probably acquired during his six years in the Marines.

"Just some jagoff detectives from the carjacking task force that somehow got here ahead of us."I responded.

"Carjacking? "The Sgt. Roared This is not some fucking carjacking unless they're stealing them from lawyers offices now. And they should know better. Where the hell did they find these guys?"

"I was wondering that myself Corbin." I said with a laugh. "Just let us know what you find."

"Will do Jack." Maris said disappearing into the offices of Giordano, Greenberg and Collins.

Outside on the street I told attorney Collins that he would be notified, when we were finished with the crime scene. I also suggested that he let an officer follow him home and clear his apartment in River North before going inside. He nodded in agreement, and I made the arrangements.

Elaine and I drove back to the station on N. Larrabee St. and on the way my phone buzzed. It was my old partner, Vernon Johnson. He had been keeping tabs on the Billy Sims case and wanted me to know that the closing arguments were going on as we spoke, and that he heard that Judge Hogan intended to instruct the jury after the arguments concluded and then had to adjourn for some reason. The jury would be brought back to deliberate in the morning. He intended to go down to 26th and California and wanted to know if I would like to be there.

It wasn't unusual for detectives to attend part of the trials in their cases and especially jury verdicts and sentencings. I told Vernon that I was pretty busy, but would like to be there and asked him to call me when he heard that the jury had reached a verdict. He said that he would, and we hung up.

Back in the detectives' room Elaina suggested that we call the FBI and make an appointment as soon as we could with the agents handling the Victor Kirilenko investigation. She made the call and made an appointment at their offices for the next day, Wednesday morning at 9 AM.

We proceeded to busy ourselves with some of our many cases until the day flew by, and as the sun started to set we decided to wrap things up for the day.

Chapter 10

At 5 AM Wednesday morning I was woken by the buzz of my cell phone on my nightstand. It took me a few seconds to focus, but when I did, I saw my dad's name and number looking back at me on my screen. So I answered.

"Hi dad. Are you okay?" My mind immediately went to the events and threats from the barbeque.

"Sure Jack. I'm fine. I just wanted to check in on you. With my trial going on I haven't been able to talk to you since Sunday. But my trial is winding down. The jury went out yesterday and will be back at it this morning."

"That sounds good dad. Our case against Billy Sims is at about the same stage. I may go down to 26th and Cal later, if we get a verdict. Vernon Johnson is going to keep me informed."

"Hey Jack, why don't you swing by and check in on me, after you finish up. Maybe we can grab lunch."

"Okay. If I get down there, I'll look in on you."

Since I was already wide-awake at 5:15 AM, I decided to go for a run down to Montrose Beach and take a swim. Leaving the Covington at 5:30 it was still dark, but by the time I got to the lake the dawn was breaking with layers of pink and dark blue in the eastern sky.

The air was warm but the oppressive humidity had broken, and the dry September air was a welcome change. I kicked off my shoes and pulled off my shirt and walked directly into Lake Michigan. The cool water felt refreshing, and the short 50 yard swim was relaxing, allowing my mind to wander for a short while away from homicide, threats and troubling contradictions.

On my way down to the beach I had looked around half hoping to see Emma Merlin's bicycle, but of course, she and her bike weren't around. Now, I wondered where she might be, and what art projects she was working on. Somehow, it was because she knew absolutely nothing about the work that I do, that I felt a real need to talk to her about it. I had to laugh at myself and decided to swim further out.

After about 1/2 hour I swam back in and took my shoes and shirt up to the grass in the park and got the sand off my feet. I finished my run back to the Covington apartments and my usual morning routine.

By 7:30 I was on the road dressed in a navy blue light weight suit with a blue Oxford short-sleeved shirt and a navy tie with green stripes. I put the top down on the Camaro and the soft September air felt amazing. I needed this little time away, but when I pulled into the station parking lot, I knew that it was back to the reality of my job and who I was and who I had always wanted to be.

I beat Elaina into work for one of the few times and went to my desk and started replying to emails and phone calls. Then the preliminary CSI report came in, and it didn't reveal too much. There were no shell casings, and most of the fingerprints were matched to Detectives Anderson and Solar as well as attorney Matt Giordano. More Prints would be checked against the other lawyers and office staff after they obtained them. The ME's Office reported that the cause of death was the gunshot to the temple and the manner was homicide. Nothing strange there. It seems Giordano died sometime Labor Day morning and had eaten shrimp scampi with linguine and garlic bread the night before. There were no drugs and only trace alcohol in his system.

Elaina came in at 8:30 a little late for her and explained that her daughter, Rosie, had stayed home from school so she had to wait for her mother who lives nearby to come over and look after her.

She jumped on her computer and worked at the keyboard for about 15 minutes, until it was time to get our car and leave for our meeting at the FBI offices on W. Roosevelt Rd.

After a 15 minute drive largely heading southwest on Ogden Avenue we pulled into the parking area beside the 10 story modern glass and steel Chicago Headquarters of the FBI. We checked in at the lobby security desk, passed through the metal detectors and were directed to the elevators. Our FBI escort told us that Special Agent Anthony Wright was expecting us on the seventh floor.

Exiting the elevator, we encountered another reception desk were a pleasant middle-aged lady named Florence sat typing something on her computer and after looking up a few seconds later let us know that Agent Wright would be with us in a moment.

Seconds later a very tall and slender guy with short-cropped brown hair strode toward us. He introduced himself, and his handshake totally engulfed mine. He invited us to follow him to his office, and when we walked in, we had quite a surprise.

Sitting behind one of the two desks in the office was the familiar and welcoming face of Special Agent Teresa Marek. She jumped up smiling broadly and rushed over to greet us. We exchanged warm handshakes and inquiries about our well-being before settling down to business.

Before we did though, I had to ask Teresa about her former partner Henry Chan. She informed us that Henry had wanted to get out of the gang related investigations for some time and finally was assigned to the kidnapping team in early August. He was still in Chicago, but she hadn't seen him since he made the move.

"Well as you both know we have the lead on attorney Cheryl Greenberg's murder. We have been looking at different motives and possible perpetrators. During the course of our investigation we were given several boxes of files by one of Greenberg's partners, Matt Giordano. And, as you may have heard, attorney Giordano was found murdered in his office yesterday morning. The ME says he was killed sometime Labor Day morning. What brought us to you was what Elaina found in one of the boxes."

I looked at my partner and she continued. "Cheryl Greenberg's personal files and notes make it clear that her client Victor Kirilenko was heavily involved in a large-scale car theft and car- jacking operation based in and around Ukrainian Village and some other Northwest side neighborhoods. That's bad enough, but he apparently was also involved with the Russian mob and some kind of radical white supremacist group calling themselves the first patriots. Then within a short period of time, Kirilenko, Greenberg and Giordano all are taken out as well as a guy who was a witness to the Greenberg murder. We are hoping you can help us put this together.

Special Agent Anthony Wright responded. "I think we can help you out detectives. Kirilenko was definitely a major player in the car theft operation, and they are a dangerous bunch in their own right with connections to violent Russian gangsters. But these First Patriot wackos are a different breed. They are totally fanatical and don't really care about money except how it helps them promote their sick ideas."

"That's an odd partnership." I noted. "The Russians and other carjacking gangs don't usually have any agenda other than making money. The young kids that are out there jacking cars are mostly involved with their own local street gangs or are doing it for kicks on the spur of the moment. These white racist types wouldn't have anything to do with them normally."

"You're right Jack." Teresa Marek chimed in. "We are fairly sure the first patriots are directly involved in the actual car thefts. We believe that they are working with the Russians in some way as far as storing them and possibly selling them off wholesale somehow. We are working on finding out exactly where the cars are going. In the meantime, we can let you in on what we have so far, if you to have some time."

Elaina and I were anxious to hear what they had, and spent the next couple of hours going over information the FBI had accumulated in the past couple of months. Around 11 AM my cell buzzed, and I looked to see a text from Vernon Johnson stating that they expected the jury to come in with a verdict soon. I thanked him, and said I would be right there.

I told the group about the text and Elaina suggested that I take our vehicle, and that she would get back to the station after finishing with the agents.

Teresa Marek assured Elaina that they would give her a ride back if needed, and I thanked them and took the key fob from my partner and hurried out to the Blazer. The drive to 26th and California was only about 12 minutes so I pulled into the parking lot and scurried across California Avenue and into the old courthouse. I quietly slipped into the courtroom and was able to sit next to Vernon Johnson. He whispered that the jury was on its way in, and sure enough they started to file into the courtroom somberly.

I have seen quite a few juries deliver verdicts in the past and they always looked serious. Sometimes they looked at the prosecutors, and we always felt that meant a conviction. Other times they glanced over at the defense table, and we usually felt that was good for the defendant meaning an acquittal or a hung jury. These jurors did neither. They all either looked straight ahead or down somewhere. Every time though the tension was palpable.

Judge Hogan asked the foreperson of the jury to rise. A middle-aged dark-haired woman nervously stood up. "Has the jury reached a verdict?" The judge inquired.

"Yes your honor," the foreperson responded. "Your Honor, on the first count of forcible rape we find the defendant not guilty."

At that there was a murmur in the crowd, and Billy Sims who was standing alongside of Linda Prassas grabbed his attorney's arm and squeezed it.

"On the second count of first-degree murder we find the defendant guilty."

Billy Sims nearly collapsed into attorney Prassas arms, and there were some cries of anguish from the group of his supporters sitting behind the defendant's table.

Judge Kate Hogan ordered quiet in the courtroom, and Sim's supporters quieted down, while he struggled to remain standing. At the prosecutor's table Terrance Goggins was beaming and shaking hands with his entire staff except notably the number two attorney in the case, Paige Owira, who busied herself putting files into her briefcase.

The judge then asked the lawyers for available dates in October for sentencing. After several dates were considered, and they agreed that the week before Halloween worked, she adjourned the case until then.

Billy Sims was being held without bail and was taken out of the courtroom in handcuffs by some Cook County deputies. Linda Prassas looked about as forlorn as a person could, while attorney Goggins strutted around like a peacock and Paige Owira remained in her chair.

Usually when there had been guilty pleas or verdicts in our cases my partner, Vernon Johnson, and I were elated. It was the culmination of a lot of hard work, and what we live for. But, for me this one felt different. I was stuck in neutral. I didn't know how to feel, and I could tell by the look on my former partner's face that he was in the same boat.

Detective Vernon Johnson was a man of few words in general, but this time he didn't say a thing. He just shook his head, patted me the shoulder and walked slowly out of the courtroom.

I looked around the room and almost everyone had left. But attorney Owira was still sitting at her table. She turned around in her seat and looked at me in a way that drew me to her like a magnet.

"You look about as happy as I am with the outcome of this case" I said quietly.

She nodded but couldn't muster a smile. "We really need to talk detective."

"Please call me Jack." I responded.

"Okay. Jack. Will you meet me tonight after work?"

"Sure. I can do that. What you have in mind?"

"Meet me at Beatniks on Chicago Avenue in West Town at six." She said. "I have to get back to the office. Goggins and the others will expect me to join in their little celebration. I'd rather jump off the Dearborn Street bridge into the river." And, at that she picked up her briefcase and walked out. My eyes were riveted.

I snapped out of it and remembered my dad's trial and went to the fourth floor and found his courtroom. Outside there were a number of lawyers and spectators sitting on benches and milling around the hallway. My dad was talking to one of his assistant attorneys that I knew, so I walked up and joined them.

"Hi there Jack. Glad you could make it down here. How did your case go?" He asked.

"We won but it doesn't feel that way. This is not good dad. Things don't seem so black-and-white today."

"You'll figure it out son." He replied with an understanding smile. "Life is complicated. Everything doesn't always move in a straight line. Just think about how you love the Cubs. Then try to answer the question why." He laughed and then his face turned serious, as a court officer approached.

"We have a verdicts attorney Fallon." The officer said and then he announced that everyone needed to go into the courtroom now!

Inside, I sat next to some cops and detectives and watched another jury walk into court. This group was in stark contrast to the Billy Sims jury. They seemed relaxed, and some of them actually smiled at the defense table.

Judge John Eggleston, an older guy of around 60 years, went through the process and the jury foreperson a young man announced that the defendant Leon Harris has been found not guilty on all charges.

The defendant shook hands with my father and attorney Alicia Kagan, as his supporters rejoiced behind them. I didn't know a thing about the case, but I couldn't help but feel good for the family and feel proud of my dad. He believed in the justice system and always said "the case wins or loses. I just do my part." I waved at him as I went on my way back to the station to do mine.

Chapter 11

After putting in several productive hours of work with Elaina at the station, I decided to go back to my apartment for a quick change of clothes before meeting Paige Owira in West Town. Traffic was heavy going outbound on Lakeshore Drive, but I was still able to get home by 5:45 PM. This gave me time to relax a little and change into a brown crewneck T-shirt, khaki slacks and a tan windbreaker.

I had just sat down on my couch listening to some tunes and enjoying the view from the 12th floor, when my phone buzzed, and it was my dad. This surprised me, since we had just talked earlier and although we were close, it wasn't like him to be calling a lot just to talk.

"What's going on dad?" I asked."Is everything okay?"

There was a pause."Not really Jack. That's why I called. There have been more serious threats made just within the last couple of hours. They have been directed at me and several of my attorneys. Don't get me wrong. Defense lawyers are used to the animosity that often comes from our own clients. It has always puzzled me, why so many defendants aim their anger at the people working the hardest to help them. But, these threats are very different. They're not coming from disgruntled clients. They are vile and angry to a fanatical degree."

"That's terrible dad. Did the threats come in over the phone like the ones at your house?"

"No. This time they were emails sent directly to me and the other attorneys from our office. They seemed to be very upset about the verdicts in my case. But, Linda Prassas is getting them too, and she lost her case. They are threatening to kill her, if she files an appeal on the Billy Sims conviction and makes up some lies for that black guy. They used a different word, but I hate even saying it. I need to tell you that Sims told her that the prosecutor cross examining him had used the N word. And that is what caused him to snap."

"Yeah. I was there when that happened. It did look like Goggins said something to him, but I couldn't hear it or read his lips. Do you think that really happened dad?"

Again there was a pause. "Well I can't be sure. We all know that defendants sometimes lie to their attorneys, but I am certain that Sims told her that. Linda Prassas is one of the most honest and dedicated lawyers that I know. I would absolutely vouch for her integrity."

"What can I do to help, dad? Do you want me to come and stay with you for a while. I don't mind it at all. It wouldn't be a problem."

"Thanks Jackie but there's no need. I reported the threats, and there will be some added patrols around my house and the homes of the others who have gotten threats. You have enough on your plate son. Concentrate on taking care of yourself."

"Okay dad. You too."

Relaxing on the couch no longer seem to be an option, so I turned off the tunes and decided to head out to Beatniks on Chicago Avenue near Ashland Avenue. I drove West on Lawrence, turned left on Ashland to Chicago and found a parking spot a few doors down from Beatniks.

When I walked inside, I was hit with an overload of colors of mismatching rugs, furniture and a an array of chandeliers. The eclectic room was filled with large plants giving the place an almost tropical feel, and the hip music was something like Motown meets Brazil 66.

I spotted Paige sitting at a table covered by funky red and teal striped canopy and a large tropical plant. Her exotic beauty seemed to blend perfectly into our surroundings, and when she smiled at me, I melted into the chair across from her and found myself at a loss for words. She was stunning, dressed in a purple tank top that didn't leave too much for the imagination and white formfitting pants.

"I am so glad you could make it Detective Fallon. I wasn't sure you would come. "She said in her warm velvety voice. "I really need someone to talk to, and it is hard to know who to trust. Somehow, I trust you."

It took me a few seconds to get my mind off of how attractive she was and remember the serious nature of what had been going on. "I'm very happy to be here and, I'm flattered that you feel you can trust me. There are so many things going on with me right now that my head is spinning. Please tell me how I can help you, and please call me Jack."

"Okay. Here goes." She took a deep breath, and her expression became serious and her voice became hushed. "There have been some things going on in the State's Attorney's Office that are frightening the hell out of me. It started for me when I noticed irregularities with the way some of the prosecutors were handling witnesses. At first, I chalked it up to overzealous Assistant State's Attorneys putting the facts in the best light possible. I even tried to convince myself at times that some of my colleagues had just misinterpreted the statements given to police officers by witnesses. But it kept happening, and it was only a few of the same lawyers doing it repeatedly. It's because I saw, how you handled Terrance Goggins at the Billy Sims trial that I felt I could trust you. You were straight with the facts. You were honest."

"Yeah. When Goggins tried to steer me into misstating the facts, I was confused. I didn't want to think it was intentional. I wasn't sure what to think. I have always trusted the prosecutors. As detectives we need to have a good working relationship with the State's Attorney's Office. But I have to say, Terrence Goggins has always made me a little uneasy. Up until the Sims trial I just figured it was because I thought he was a jerk. Then after what I witnessed during his cross-examination, I had serious questions. I could tell he said something under his breath to Sims, but couldn't hear what it was."

"That's the problem Jack. I could see Goggins clearly, when he turned his back on the jury and saw the judge looking down at her notes. He said fuck you nigger to Sims. I had no doubt. It was shocking to me. All this time working with him and not really knowing him. I can only imagine what he thinks and says about me."

"Oh shit! I was trying not to believe it. Sims lawyer, Linda Prassas told my dad that Billy Sims told her that Goggins had done that to him. It made him lose it and go after him. It may have also caused him to get convicted for a murder he didn't commit. This is beyond awful. "

Our server came by and briefly interrupted our train of thought. We decided on a bottle of wine, and I let Paige choose. She ordered an Argentinian Chardonnay. I suggested that we have some small plates. and she let me take the lead. I went for West Coast oysters, calamari and ceviche.

"I don't know what to do. If I report it, Goggins will deny it, and I will have to present myself as an expert lip reader. My career would be over, and things could get rough. I'm actually afraid Jack. Do you think I'm overreacting? "

I saw the sorrowful look on Paige's face and wanted to hug her, but controlled myself." No. I don't think you're overreacting. In fact, my father and some of his attorneys have been getting serious threats. And that includes Linda Prassas. She got an email specifically warning her not to file an appeal for Sims making up lies about what happened in court. My dad said she intends to file a notice of appeal tomorrow."

"That doesn't surprise me." Paige responded." Prassas is a good lawyer, and appeals in any serious criminal case are pretty standard after a conviction. I'm afraid of where this may go Jack. If it comes down to it, I won't lie. The choice would be made for me. I really need some time to think. I am so glad you're here. I really need to be with someone right now."

She reached across the table and placed her hand into mine causing a warm sensual arousal to surge throughout my entire body.

Just then our server, Melissa, arrived with our wine and oysters. "I hope I'm not spoiling the mood." She said with a knowing smile. Looks like the oysters and wine were a good idea."

Paige slowly removed her hand from mine causing another ripple of electricity to flow through me. "I have to tell you that this morning I had a strong urge to talk about all of this with a friend who doesn't know anything about our work. Right now though, I can't think of anywhere I would rather be than right here with you. Let's take a break from all this dreariness and enjoy the moment for a while."

It was a pleasure to see her smile, as she reached for an oyster, and I poured our wine. Each of the oysters was covered by a wedge of some kind of tropical fruit that really provided an unusual taste to the oysters. We spent the next couple of hours eating the delicious food, drinking a second bottle of wine and telling each other about ourselves. It was magical, and the time flew by.

I learned that she had grown up in Birmingham Alabama with her mother, an African American from rural Alabama and her father, a Japanese engineer who came to Birmingham to work in the steel industry. That answered my curiosity about her unusual exotic beauty. She went to the University of Alabama and came to Chicago to attend Chicago-Kent College of Law and never left.

Melissa came by with the check, and I picked it up, but Paige playfully took it from me. "This one's on me Detective Fallon. But it's going to cost you". She asked me what I was driving and where I was parked. "Follow me to my place. I will pull around in my silver CRV. I don't live too far away."

I didn't have to be asked twice.

I followed Paige to a side street off W. Division St. and found a parking space a little past where she pulled in. With the top put up on my Camaro, I followed her into a brick two-story four flat and up the interior stairs to her second-floor apartment.

Inside, I found a clean nicely furnished front room with a typical narrow hallway leading to a bedroom, dining room, kitchen and bathroom. As she showed me around, I noticed the usual small kitchen in the back with the window over the sink looking out to a small backyard and alley. The back door had two small windowpanes and led out to a shared porch and stairs leading down to the yard.

After taking a quick glance out of the kitchen window, I turned around to find Paige standing so close to me that as soon as I moved slightly forward, our bodies were pressed together. The way she looked at me was so inviting that I didn't hesitate. We engaged in a long sensuous kiss. The way her tongue felt and tasted, it was game over.

She took my hand and led me into her bedroom. She didn't bother turning on a light and proceeded to peel her clothes off in an instant. I wasn't far behind, and we embraced and continued kissing. Her brown skin was silky smooth including her small but perfectly rounded behind. I was immediately at full erection and picked her up and gently placed her on the bed. I followed and began licking her black pointed nipples on her firm natural breasts.

She began breathing heavily and moaning a little. I moved my mouth down her stomach onto her pussy which was already wet. She was fully shaved and had a clean musty taste and smell. I found her sweet spot with my tongue and her moaning grew louder, until she was begging me not to stop, and then she exploded into shuddering orgasms.

She deftly pulled my head up from her and asked me to kiss her. I was happy to oblige and after more deep wet kissing, she opened her legs and said that she wanted me inside her.

Placing my throbbing cock inside her I was overwhelmed by how moist and warm it felt. I had to concentrate on not coming too soon, and her loud moaning made it harder to keep from releasing a torrent of sperm.

She liked it slow and comfortable, so after about 10 minutes of rhythmically moving in and out of her, I erupted and enjoyed a fantastic release. She was now much wetter than she already had been.

After a couple of enchanting minutes, I pulled off of her and we just laid next to each other awash in an awesome afterglow. We chatted for a while as lovers do, and then I became hard again and began kissing and caressing her. She said that she wanted to ride me and rolled over straddling me and placing me easily inside of her wide open vagina.

She liked to move up and down and occasionally lean all the way down to kiss me, at which time I placed both of my hands on her beautiful ass and started pumping. She kept kissing and moaning until I came again with almost as much delivery as the first time.

After another pause in the afterglow, I reached under her buttocks and turned her over. The view of her from behind got me going again, and she got up on all fours and reached back to guide me into her. It was great moving in and out of her while pressing into her beautifully rounded behind. I held onto her breasts while rhythmically moving in and out, until we both yelled and came at the same time.

This time the afterglow turned into a deep sleep. When I awoke it was 4:30 AM and I realized that I had to get home. I quietly put on my clothes and leaned over and kissed her in the back of her neck. It wasn't easy to leave her. Out on the leafy quiet Street it was a comfortable temperature, and it seemed so serene almost obscuring the simple complexity of this magnificently confounding city.

Chapter 12

I got back to my apartment around 5 AM and realized that the couple of hours of sleep I had that night weren't nearly enough. I was exhausted. I sent Elaina a text alerting her that my arrival at work today would be a little late. I set my phone alarm to 8:30 and quickly fell into a deep sleep on top of my bed covers.

The alarm seemed to come only seconds later, and it took me several minutes to focus enough to get up and on my feet. There was no time for most of my morning ritual, only a shave, a shower and a glass of orange juice on the way out the door.

By the time I walked through the door of the detectives' room it was 9:15 AM and the place was buzzing. All of the detectives seemed to be heading out on a call, and Elaina stood up from her desk and said in a commanding voice "let's go Jack. I'll explain on the way."

On the way where, I thought to myself, but I didn't question my partner. I simply followed her out to the carpool and got into the passenger seat of a gray Chevy Impala, as Detective Rodriguez took her place in the driver seat.

"A 36-year-old woman named Rachel Braun was shot in the head a few minutes ago in River North during a carjacking. Lieut. Whitchead came into the detectives' room five minutes ago and gave us the case. I told him you had just ran out to Dunkin' Donuts." She said while crossing herself. "Dios min Thank God you got here when you did amigo."

We flew out of the lot with lights on and siren blaring. "Sorry partner." I said. "I had a meeting with one of the prosecutors from the Sims case last night, and it turned into something much more complicated than I expected. I didn't get home until 5 AM"

"I see." Elaina replied with a wry smile. "What is her name?"

"It's not what you think." I responded. "I mean, it is what you think, but it really was one of the prosecutors. Her name is Paige Owira. She had some concerns about the case. Actually some things that bother me too. I don't know for sure where this is going, but the fact that it's becoming something much more personal scares the hell out of me!"

That train of thought was stopped in its tracks, as we turned off N. Orleans St. and parked in front of a condo complex which was already surrounded by patrol cars, an ambulance and a fire truck. The EMTs were just loading a gurney into the ambulance, as we jumped out of our car and ran up to them.

"Hold on!" I yelled loudly. They stopped just short of placing her into the ambulance. I can see that the woman with short dark brown hair on the gurney was conscious and alert. Her dark brown eyes stared right through me. "Are you able to speak?" I asked. Her mouth was covered by an oxygen mask, but she nodded her head yes. I turned to the EMTs. The one closest to me was a short stocky young woman with medium length dreads. "We really need to talk to her right now. Can you remove the oxygen mask for a couple of minutes?"

The young EMTs looked unsure and glanced over to a wiry middle-aged guy with short salt-and-pepper hair who took charge. "Okay detectives. I think she can handle it, but briefly. I'll give you two minutes." He gently unhooked Rachel Braun from the oxygen mask and turned off the oxygen tank. "Two minutes and that's it!"

Our victim had bandages around her head and was hooked up to a bag of plasma. It was clear that she had a head wound and had just lost a lot of blood. I was amazed that she was able to speak, but there was no time to waste. "Did you see who did this to you?" I asked.

"Yes. This man came up to me and grabbed my purse off my shoulder as I approached my car. I screamed at him and grabbed a hold of my bag, but he pushed me away. He threatened to kill me and called me a bitch. He was swearing and threatening, but I was pissed off. I kept fighting with him, until he pulled out a gun and shot me. I guess the shot knocked me out. He probably thought I was dead."

"Do you remember anything about him?" Elaina asked.

"He was in his 30s or early 40s, around 6 feet tall and average build. He had sandy colored scruffy hair and pale blue eyes."

I could see the male EMT give us the sign to cut the interview off. "Anything else you can think of?"

She paused. "Oh yeah. The man spoke with some kind of southern accent. I'm not too good with that kind of thing, but it definitely wasn't Chicago.

That was all we got, but it was better than nothing. Rachel Braun was hooked back up to the oxygen, loaded into the ambulance and on her way to Northwestern Memorial Hospital. Just as the EMTs pulled away, an unmarked police car drove up and took the same parking spot.

Emerging from the blue Ford Fusion sedan were task force Detectives Roger O'Brien and Carl Nijinsky. I couldn't help wondering how the Task Force guys who are covering the whole Northside kept showing up so quickly to our crime scenes. At least it wasn't Detectives Anderson and Solar, I thought to myself.

O'Brien and Nijinsky approached us and greeted us amicably. It was noticeably different than how their fellow task force detectives carried themselves. "What have we got here Jack?" O'Brien asked.

I proceeded to relate everything that we knew at that point. Nijinsky took a few notes, and they both seemed genuinely appreciative." Thanks for the info guys." O'Brien said." We will stay out of your way. We know the drill. Homicide has the priority. We won't bother your witness. She has enough to deal with. Just keep us in the loop. We have plenty of other cases to close down."

"No problem detectives." I responded." It's a pleasure dealing with professionals."

I can see that hit a chord with both O'Brien and Nijinsky. I went on to explain our uncomfortable experience with Detectives Anderson and Solar at the crime scene inside the law offices of Giordano, Greenberg and Collins.

"Sorry to hear that. "O'Brien said with a grimace."Those two guys don't represent how most of the task force detectives operate. If they give you any trouble, let us know. We will take care of it."

"Yeah we'll straighten them out for you, if you want," Nijinsky added.

At that Elaina bristled. "That is not necessary. We know how to handle people like that."

O'Brien and Nijinsky both chuckled and got back into their car before taking a call and speeding away with lights flashing." You know, Jack, all those task force guys give me the creeps. They're very different, but creepy just the same."

"I don't know partner. I don't have any problem with these two guys." I answered." The other two are a different story."

My phone buzzed, and I answered a call from Special Agent Teresa Marek." Detective Fallon, your Lieutenant called our office about 15 minutes ago and informed us about the carjacking and attempted murder of Rachel Braun. We were able to track her Maxima through its GPS system to Ukrainian Village. We are heading over there right now. Can you join us? "

"Absolutely!" I responded. "We will head right over there. We aren't too far away." I informed Elaina and she went straight to our car, and I was right behind her.

Elaina drove north to Division Street and headed west. As we approached Damon Avenue, Agent Marek called back." Jack, we are tracking the Maxima, and it just turned off Western Avenue going east on Augusta Boulevard. We're driving a silver Ford Taurus. Where are you guys?"

"We are going West on Division Street in a gray Impala. We can go down to Augusta and continue west. Our paths should cross in a couple of minutes." Elaina heard me and took the first left down to Augusta and then turned right. Two blocks down I spotted a silver Taurus pulled over on the other side of the street and told Elaina to take the first parking spot.

As soon as she pulled over to the curb, Marek called." I don't know what the hell happened. We were only a couple blocks away and it just disappeared. The signal stopped right around here. Did you notice a green Maxima anywhere?"

We definitely hadn't seen a green Maxima. I suggested that we cover the neighborhood for a while looking for the car or a likely place it could have pulled into. There was already a BOLO out on the Maxima, but I called dispatch and asked for an alert for the Ukrainian Village and West Town neighborhoods

We spent the next hour and 1/2 crisscrossing the area passing the FBI agents and several patrol cars but saw no green Maxima. There were a number of gas stations and several auto repair shops in the neighborhood. We took the gas stations, and the agents took the repair shops. Without warrants all we could do was ask a few questions and look from the outside. We didn't see the Maxima or anything that gave us a reason to go any further.

I asked Elaina, if she was hungry, and she definitely was ready for lunch. I knew of a good authentic Ukrainian place in the neighborhood, and my partner was anxious to try it. Marek called to report basically the same lack of results. But they were happy to join us for lunch, and she was familiar with the Old Lviv Ukrainian Restaurant on W. Chicago Ave.

A few minutes later Elaina pulled the Impala into a parking spot in front of the blue awnings with gold lettering hanging over the inviting windows which provided a look into the old world Ukrainian restaurant. Shortly thereafter, Agents Tony Wright and Teresa Marek arrived, and we walked in together.

We were greeted by a plump middle-aged woman with shoulder length blonde hair and bright blue eyes. Her accent was thick, but seemed perfectly appropriate for the old school European atmosphere. The lady, named Mariana, seated us at a table near a white painted wall, decorated with tapestry seemingly made from wood or bark containing old world depictions of structures and animals as well as wooden plates and imitation gas lanterns. Our table which could easily seat six people was covered by a white tablecloth with a variety of Brown decorative stripes.

Mariana took our drink orders of coffee and pop and then said something to us that was unintelligible to me. Teresa Marek responded in kind, and a lively conversation ensued between the FBI agent and our host. Elaina and I looked at each other and then at Agent Marek.

"Hey, how many languages do you speak, Teresa?" Elaina asked.

"Only five fluently." She responded. "But, I have a passing knowledge of quite a few more. Mariana and I were speaking Ukrainian. Interestingly, she speaks it with a Russian accent like my mother who was born in eastern Ukraine where there are many Russian-speaking Ukrainians. Many people in those regions speak both Ukrainian and Russian, and they sometimes use both in conversation. So, I grew up in a household with my Polish father and Ukrainian speaking mother. I am fluent in Ukrainian, but can get by with Polish and Russian."

"Wow! Who knew?" I exclaimed, as Agent Wright laughed and Teresa Marek just smiled looking coy.

Mariana invited us to help ourselves to the hot buffet. Teresa informed us. "It smells great! Let's go!"

We helped ourselves to an array of perogies, varenyky dumplings, stuffed cabbages and soups including borscht.

After enjoying the amazing, sumptuous meal and some pleasant conversation, we focused on the serious business that brought us to Ukrainian Village. Elaina and I explained our focus was on the homicides of Matt Giordano, Cheryl Greenberg and Jay Farrell as well as the attempted murder of Rachel Braun. But we were aware of the possible connections to the carjacking problem and the question, of how the threats from racial hate groups could be involved.

Agents Wright and Marek were understandably working on big picture issues, involving radical hate groups and how they recruit members, raise money and engage in violence that threatens individuals and the entire fabric of our country. They were aware of a radical anarchist group calling themselves the first patriots that was begun in the Chicago area a few years back, and that used white supremacist dogma to recruit almost entirely young and middle-aged white men in the Midwest. There have been some indications that their recruitment had expanded recently to some southern states.

"Have you seen any changes or increase in their activities in recent months?", I interjected.

"We definitely have. "Agent Wright responded. "There has been a big jump in their presence on social networks and websites promoting racism and conspiracy theories of all kinds. They have been recruiting by promising a chance to join an army of patriots that will be heavily armed and ready to take down the enemy's of the white race. We are taking these guys very seriously and have been looking at ways to monitor them more closely. They have been communicating with elements of the Russian mob up here in Chicago. We are working on that angle to."

"Any specifics on their use of terroristic threats?", I inquired. "Greenberg and Giordano were getting threats before they were killed, and threats have been directed toward my father and some of the defense lawyers he works with. I am worried about it."

"We are aware that there has been an uptick in reports of serious threats directed at lawyers and even judges in the Chicago area. We can't comment on the specific reports that we have received, but we are aware of your situation Jack. We will keep you posted as much as we can." Agent Marek assured me.

Before I could respond, my phone buzzed. It was Lieut. Whitehead. "Fallon, you and Rodriguez need to get over to the Gold Coast right now! Judge John Eggleston has just been murdered in his home on Goethe Street. You and Rodriguez are on the lead. This may be connected to Greenberg and Giordano. Get going!"

Chapter 13

The FBI agents went on their way, and in less than 10 minutes we were parked on Goethe Street in the Gold Coast neighborhood, where Elaina and I had closed the Chinese Trade Consulate case less than two months earlier. The street was buzzing with squad cars, an ambulance and unmarked police cars.

I spotted Lieut. Whitehead standing outside of a three-story brownstone townhouse talking to some EMTs who were leaving the scene empty-handed. He turned around as we approached him. "Okay detectives here's what we've got. Apparently, some guy dressed in a hard hat and phone company linesman outfit came to the front door, and Judge Eggleston's wife opened it to him. Then, the guy brushed her aside and confronted the judge demanding his car fob before shooting him in the head. He was just pronounced dead on the scene. The judge happened to be home today because of a positive result from a COVID test. The Medical Examiner's Office will be here soon.

"Have you been inside, Lieutenant?" I asked.

"No one's going in except the ME and the CSI team. They will be coming all masked up. The EMTs gave Mrs. Eggleston a rapid COVID test, and will have the result in a few minutes. One of the female EMTs is in there with the judge and his wife who was understandably in shock."

"We need to get a BOLO out on the judge's car right away." Elaina offered. "Do we know the make and color and tag number?"

"We're working on that. Unfortunately, Mrs. Eggleston hasn't been able to say anything more than he shot him and took his car. She shut down after that. I have detectives Latner and Sanchez on their way here. You're going to need help, and I know you two have worked with them before. You guys are still on the lead."

Looking around the scene, I couldn't believe my eyes. Walking toward us on the sidewalk were Detectives Oscar Anderson and Jorge Solar. They were talking to uniformed officers, one of whom pointed toward the judge's townhouse, and they started walking onto the stone slab pathway leading to the front door. I saw Whitehead's eyes light up, and he grabbed the nearest uniform officer and told him to go and get those detectives and bring them to him.

Just as the odd couple detectives got to the townhouse steps, the officer stopped them and pointed toward where we were standing. The clearly disgruntled pair turned back and walked toward us.

"We're investing a car theft gentleman. We have authority here. You can't interfere with us this time Fallon." Oscar Anderson said while smilling.

This little interaction seemed to get a rise out of our Lieut. Whitehead, He stepped in front of us and growled right back. "Well maybe Detective Fallon can't, but I sure as hell can." His 6'6" frame seem to get taller and his athletic build seem to expand. "You two can drag your asses out of my crime scene. I'll let your Lieutenant know when Homicide is finished with their work here. Is that clear!"

Anderson and Solar were taken aback by Whitehead's powerful response. They started walking backwards while keeping their eyes on the still fired up Lieutenant.

"And how in the hell did you know there was a stolen car? We haven't released a BOLO yet."

"We have our sources Lieut. We'll leave it at that." Anderson offered with a sly smile. He and his partner walked back to their car and drove off. I knew that we were going to be seeing those two again.

Whitehead then also went on his way. Elaina and I organized the sealing off of the crime scene and stood by, as the judge's wife was carted off by the EMTs. She appeared to be totally in shock, and the EMTs were covering her up to keep her warm and talking to her to keep her focus on them. We knew that it would be at least hours and possibly days, before she could be interviewed.

I spotted Detectives Morgan Latner and Henrique Sanchez arriving in a dark blue Chevy Malibu sedan, as my phone buzzed. It was Capt. Dave Norris from the Glencoe Police Department. He let me know that there had been a burglary at the Greenberg's home that afternoon. The Greenbergs discovered it after returning home from having lunch in Glenview. Capt. Norris thought we should know, and I agreed telling him that Detective Rodriguez and I would head their way immediately.

We gave Latner and Sanchez the run down on what we knew about Judge John Eggleston's murder and asked them to take control of the crime scene. They would coordinate with the CSI team and work with uniformed officers to canvass the neighborhood. We would be in touch, when we were leaving Glencoe.

We climbed into our car with Elaina at the wheel, and we rode up Lakeshore Drive and then Sheridan Road without paying much attention to the scenery this time. We were both on edge and seriously concerned about the wave of lethal attacks against lawyers and now a judge. The threats made against members of the legal system were coming to fruition and seemed to be escalating. We both took it as a direct threat against us and everything we believed in. After all, we were part of the legal system too.

When we turned left on Park Avenue and could see a couple of Glencoe police cars parked in front of the Greenberg's house on the right, we found a spot on the street as close as we could get. Elaina needed to actually drive past the residence, turn around and park near the intersection just across from the start of Glencoe Beach Park.

Walking up to the house, we saw Capt. Norris and one of his deputies walking out of the front door. He looked at us and waved for us to come to him on the sidewalk. "All right detectives, this is what we have here." He got right to the point. "The Greenbergs came back from lunch and were alarmed to find the back door ajar. They could see that it had been damaged and immediately got back into their car and drove to the station. Good move on their part. They could've walked in on something and been in real trouble."

"Yeah good move," I agreed. "We appreciate the call, Captain. What can you tell us about the break-in? "

"Well it looks like it was a quick in and out. Whoever it was didn't bother with anything in the kitchen, living room or dining room. They went straight for the home office and the bedrooms. It was obvious that the desktop computer was taken from the office, and they were looking for something in the bedrooms. We did a walk-through with the Greenbergs, and the only thing that they knew was missing was their daughter Cheryl's laptop computer. It was in her old bedroom."

Elaine and I looked at each other. "Of course her laptop," I exclaimed. "Did you see a laptop listed on the evidence sheet or the CSI report? "

"No Jack. I didn't. That makes sense. She probably took notes at all of her interviews on her laptop including her meetings with Kirilenko."

"Captain, are the Greenbergs available? We really need to talk to them."

"I don't have a problem with that." Norris responded. "They were pretty shook up by the break-in and decided to stay with some friends for a couple of days, but they are still in Glencoe. They are visiting with the Suttles on Grove Street. I believe it's 505 Grove. You can't miss it. It's just across the street from the golf course."

After a short drive, we parked in front of the two story wood shingled colonial and walked up the brick pathway to the front double Dutch doors. Before ringing the bell, the front door opened and we were greeted by a pleasant looking middle-aged woman with salt and pepper medium length hair wearing a white pullover long sleeved shirt white pants and a colorful vest with red blue and yellow designs.

"Please come in." She said. "My name is Jane. Let's sit in the sunroom." She led us through the living room to the sun porch with sliding glass doors on three sides with screens which allowed them to open. On that day there was a nice breeze flowing through the room, and the small backyard with a couple of trees, groundcover and several flower beds made for very pleasant atmosphere.

Our host introduced us to her husband Dave Suttle and the Greenbergs who indicated that they had met us before. There were enough chairs for all of us to sit down comfortably. No one said anything for about 15 seconds. It didn't seem necessary. I could certainly see why someone would want to go to this place for comfort and relaxation.

"Thank you for seeing us so soon." Elaina said to the Greenbergs. "We know how difficult this time has been for you both, and now a break-in at your home. You have been through so much." Mr. Greenberg nodded and expressed his thanks and desire to help. He went over the day's events. There had been nothing unusual until they returned home after lunch and saw the open damaged back door. He went on to restate pretty much the same version as Capt. Norris.

"The Captain told us about the missing computers." I noted. "What can you tell us about them?"

"The desktop is a five-year-old iMac that we used primarily for family business and a little bit of social media and research once in a while. We aren't really computer people. My wife gets on the Internet occasionally and looks at her email on the computer. I don't care for it. I get some email and texts on my phone, but I keep it to a minimum."

"What about Cheryl?" Elaina asked. "Did she use it?"

"Oh no!" Mrs. Greenberg chimed in. "Cheryl was tied to her laptop since her last two years in high school. But she never used our computer. She didn't like it. She said her laptop was much faster and had apps or something."

"Why did she leave her laptop here in Glencoe?" I inquired.

"Oh that wasn't her current laptop. She kept that one more for sentimental reasons. She hasn't used it since law school." Man, I thought. We have a missing laptop, and we aren't the only ones looking for it. "Do you know if she used a password?" I continued.

"I'm sure she did." Mrs. Greenberg answered. She was like that. Very private, even as a teenager. She didn't want anyone getting into her business. We have never known her passwords."

"Do you know anyone that might have them?" Elaina asked.

There was a silence as the Greenbergs looked quizzically at each other. Then Mrs. Greenberg answered. "Possibly Patti Vail. She was her best friend in high school, and they have remained close ever since."

"Where can we find her?" I followed up.

"She lives in Evanston now. We don't have her phone number, but she works at the Michigan Shores Club in Wilmette. She is the Aquatics Director and is in charge of the pool and the swim teams. She and Cheryl were both on the swimming team at New Trier together. She might be there now. You just go back south on Sheridan Road. Take a left at the stop light just before Gilson Park and then the immediate left on Michigan Avenue. The club is right there on the corner. You can't miss it."

On the way there I called our district evidence storage desk located in the basement of our station and asked to speak to officer Sal Taglia in the storage room. Everyone called him Sarge. He was a crusty old guy that had been there for years and ruled with an iron fist.

"Sarge this is Fallon. Can you do me a favor?" I was used to treading lightly with Sarge. I've seen detectives try to rush him or pull rank on him, and it never worked out well for them.

"What the hell do you want now Detective Fallon? This ain't the damn favor room. This is the dam evidence locker. My fuckin' evidence locker!"

"Okay your highness. Just look at the Cheryl Greenberg evidence list, and tell me whether you have a laptop computer entered. You are the only man for the job. When I need a job done right, I only go to the best."

"Cut the crap Fallon. You're so full of shit it's coming out of your ears. Just hold your horses. It'll take me a minute." There was silence for a couple of minutes, and then his gravelly voice was back. "Yeah, I got the list and no there's no laptop."

"Are you sure?" I asked incredulously.

Listen kid. I said there's no damn laptop! Capisce?"

"Okay. Okay. No problem. A thousand pardons. Hey wait a minute. There is a car listed right?"

"Sure kid. There's a car listed. It's a white Lexus

"Do we have it at our impound lot?"

"Yeah we got it here. I'm surprised those other two detectives didn't ask about it."

"What other two detectives?"

"Some jagoffs named Anderson and Solari or something. A couple of real pricks. You know those guys?"

"Yeah we know them." I snapped. "We feel the same way about them that you do. Listen, if they come by again, tell them that the car was moved to another location, somewhere on the south side. I'm going to get in touch with the CSI team and have them meet us at the car. Thanks Sarge you're the greatest."

"Cut the crap Fallon!"

Chapter 14

We parked on Michigan Avenue in front of the stately English country style limestone building and entered the covered main entrance. The swimming pool was visible in front of us through a long stretch of glass panels, and to our left the reception desk was being managed by an older smiling gray-haired lady with a name tag that read Margaret.

She welcomed us warmly, and after introductions we asked to speak to Patti Vail. "Oh yes certainly. " Margaret responded. "Patti is usually getting ready for some swim lessons at this time but, oh wait. I forgot. She is off now for a few days. Patti and her husband left this morning to go camping in Wisconsin for a long weekend. She should be back to work Monday morning."

"Damn." I said catching myself before going any further. "Sorry Margaret, but it is important that we speak to her. Do you have a cell phone number for her?"

"Well, we don't normally give out any personal information like that."

Elaina took over and softly reassured the clearly conflicted woman that we think that Patti would want her to give us the number since we are investigating the death of her best friend Cheryl Greenberg. And, we have reason to believe that Patti might have vital information for us.

Elaina's words clearly had an effect. "Oh what a shame about Cheryl. I knew her when she was a young girl. They both swam here on our youth team before swimming at New Trier. I will get the number for you."

Margaret returned a minute later and happily recited Patti Vail's cell phone number. "I really hope this helps. Cheryl was such a sweet girl."

"Thanks for your help Margaret," Elaina said sincerely. On the way out we both waved to her and told her that we were going to try to give Patti a call right away.

"Okay. Good luck detectives. You probably won't be able to reach her until Monday, though. They drive way up north to go camping, and there isn't much cell service up there. Patti often says that she goes camping to get away, and she just turns the darn thing off. Nice to meet you both."

Once outside, we couldn't help but look at each other and laugh. Well, that was much ado about nothing, I couldn't help thinking. But we did enjoy meeting sweet old Margaret and visiting such a cool club. It fit right in with the neighborhood of expensive homes, beaches, parks and the nearby Baha'i Temple.

On the ride back to the reality of the 18th District Police Station, I called our CSI team and received more bad news. It seems that they were all busy processing other crime scenes and wouldn't be able to help us with Cheryl Greensburg's car until the next morning. What a shocker.

Then I got a call from Paige that didn't exactly cheer me up either. She was in quite a frenzy and needed to see me right away. I was happy to hear from her, but her tone of voice was alarming. "Jack, I just got a call from the superintendent at my building who told me that he saw a tall white guy at my back door trying to get in. He yelled at him from the second floor apartment next door where he was fixing the kitchen faucet. The guy bolted down the stairs before the super could catch up to him. He drove away in a gray or silver truck that was parked in the alley. I'm afraid to go home. Can we meet somewhere."

"Man, I don't like the sound of that. Let's meet in Uptown. You can stay with me if you want. Give me about an hour and 1/2. Meet me at the Demera Restaurant on North Broadway. This will be okay Paige. I will make sure of that."

"Okay Detective Fallon. I'll hold you to it." She said with a laugh.

By the time we got back to the station, Detectives Latner and Sanchez had returned from the Eggleston crime scene. They had undertaken a thorough canvassing of the immediate neighborhood and found a few people that had seen a middle-aged white man in some kind of a work uniform, but no one paid any attention to him. The people in the wealthy Gold Coast neighborhood are used to seeing service providers of all different stripes working in and around the apartments and townhouses that dominate the tree-lined streets. They also found a few surveillance cameras that could be useful and were working on getting the video. Latner felt that they would need to go back to further canvas Goethe Street and the surrounding blocks.

I placed a call to Agent Teresa Marek to inform her of Judge Eggleston's murder and see if they had anything new for us. She and Agent Wright were out in the field, so I left a message asking her to call my cell, whenever she got a chance.

Since we couldn't get CSI to assist us with Cheryl Greenberg's car until Friday morning and Cheryl's best friend Patti Vail wouldn't be back until Monday, we decided to dive back into the boxes of files on the Kirilenko case that Matt Giordano had given to us, before he was murdered. We uncovered a few more references to meetings Kirilenko had with police, and indications that more of attorney Greenberg's notes were contained in her laptop computer.

After a little more than an hour it was past 5 PM, and I told Elaina that I needed to meet Paige Owira in Uptown. I didn't want to say too much about it at the station, since many of the officers and detectives had close working relationships with prosecutors in the State's Attorney's Office. Elaina knew a little bit about my concerns with the Sims case and of course the threats made against us and my dad. She said that she was going to keep digging into the files and would see me in the morning.

I felt like I was running a little late to meet Paige at the Demera Ethiopian Restaurant in my neighborhood. My mind kept reliving the night we had just spent together, and I couldn't help feeling physically and emotionally excited to see her. The physical arousal didn't surprise me, but the emotional feelings did. Ever since I had broken off my long term relationship with Gina Gulliano after five years, an emotional commitment was far from my mind.

When I walked into the place, she was sitting at a white tableclothed table for two near the cream-colored wall decorated with classic paintings of ancient countryside settings. The floor was made of dark wood panels and the chairs were wooden and painted black. It felt warm and exotic, but Paige overshadowed it all even while dressed in a conservative black lawyer's skirt and jacket.

She stood up and greeted me with a warm embrace that pressed herself against me so closely that I couldn't hide my arousal and anyway I didn't want to. We both reluctantly pulled back and sat down. I was falling for her, and I wasn't going to try to stop it.

"I am so glad to see you Jack. I know that I could be overreacting, but I have been a wreck all day. With everything going on and now more threats, the thought of some guy hanging around my back door just freaked me out."

"Wait a minute, Paige. What do you mean more threats?", I asked.

"When I got to the office this morning, there was a message printed out on computer paper telling me to remember which side I was on or suffer the consequences. It said I needed to stay away from Detective Fallon and his traitorous criminal loving father and his bunch of traitor defense lawyers. It said "we have our eyes on all the players in the legal system. Lawyers, cops and even judges are all fair game. We are the First Patriots, and we are starting here in Chicago. We will decide who are the ones legally representing our laws and justice, and who will be legally dead.""

I tried not to look as worried as I felt. This was more than troubling to me. Either someone working at the State's Attorney's Office left that threatening letter, or someone was able to get in there and drop it off. Since there was no way to know who to trust in her office, I advised her to let me keep the printout and not to mention it to anyone else for now. I wanted her to act as normal as possible, but to be as careful as possible.

Our server, a middle-aged dark woman with tied back black hair and a strong accent that I imagined to be Ethiopian stopped by and introduced herself as Amara. She brought waters, and asked us what else we would like to drink.

Paige raised her hand and suggested that we try the house made honey wine. I liked the idea, but would have gone along with anything that brought a smile to her face at that point. We also ordered some chicken dumpling appetizers and did our best to lighten the mood and enjoy the evening.

After finishing the bottle of honey wine and the dumplings, we ordered a seafood and lamb and tray to share and a bottle of South African Sauvignon Blanc. We were both able to relax and talk about our lives and everything and anything other than the threats and hateful people. We topped our dinner off with Coffee and shared an Ethiopian style tiramisu.

This time Paige let me take the bill and I said, "Now you have to follow me home tonight."

"You drive a hard bargain so to speak, detective." She said laughingly. "Lead the way. I'm all yours."

She followed me into the parking area of the Covington Apartments, and I directed her into a visitor's spot. We took the elevator up to my 12th floor apartment. The view over Lincoln Park and Lake Michigan revealed the soft twilight of dusk. I switched on my sound system to an easy listening station, and when I turned around Paige had completely disrobed and gently removed my jacket and unbuttoned my shirt and untied my tie while kissing me softly. I took care of my pants with my Beretta and Star on the belt.

Paige took me by the hand and led me into the bedroom where we entered into a hot sensual lovemaking that lasted well into the night, before we fell asleep in each other's arms. It was magical and for that moment there was no fear or worry only sweet dreams.

Chapter 15

As I awoke and opened my eyes, it seemed as though Paige was opening her's at the exact same time. The closeness I was feeling was surprising and troubling. It was something that I was sure I didn't really want after breaking it off with Gina. Now things weren't so clear to me.

The urge to make love to her was beginning to rise within me, but it was time to go to work for both of us. So, I hopped out of bed and told Paige that I would shower first. Once the water was warm enough I stepped in and squeezed some shampoo into my hand and began lathering my hair. My eyes closed and I put my head directly under the shower.

Before the rinsing was finished, I felt her body pressed upon me. Every part of her melted into me as she reached around and began stroking my cock and my balls. I turned and placed my hands under her firm behind and picked her up to me. Work would have to wait for a little while. She seemed so light as she wrapped her arms around my neck and kissed me deeply. I slid myself into her easily and pressed her gently against the wall as I rhythmically moved in and nearly all of the way out, until we came together, and she gave out a sweet moan that I had grown to love hearing. We were now both wet all over.

Paige washed her hair which resulted in lathering us both and we washed each other in a wonderful afterglow that we only reluctantly terminated in favor of the realities of our jobs.

While dressing, we chatted about the work we each had that day, and attorney Owira informed me that she had been reassigned to a new team at the State's Attorney's Office working on major crimes including carjacking. The unit was headed by Senior Attorney, Tara Thistle. Paige was also working with another young attorney named Jason Smith and had just been given a carjacking case that was heading for trial.

I thought that was an interesting coincidence and told Paige that I would like to hear more about it later. She was given a basic outline of my day, and we each settled for a glass of orange juice and some wheat toast for breakfast.

By around 7:30 AM we went down to the parking area and I followed her to her apartment in Wicker Park. People had started going to work, and there were some open spaces on the street near her apartment building. We entered the front vestibule where she collected her mail before opening the downstairs door leading to the staircase and up to her second- floor apartment across from her one upstairs neighbor.

The security in the front seemed pretty good. The building used a standard buzz in system with an intercom which is common in many older Chicago apartment buildings. Her front door was solid and had the usual doorknob lock, a deadbolt and a chain. Pretty standard stuff. While she changed clothes, I took a look at her kitchen and back door. There were no signs of damage to the door on the outside or any tampering with the small window above the sink or either of the two small windows on the top half of the back door. The landing and the stairs in back were visible to her neighbor as was the small backyard and alley. The Wicker Park area was generally safe, but under the circumstances the whole situation made me nervous about her safety. I was glad to know that she was packing a travel bag for the next few days.

I walked Paige to her car, got into my Camaro and headed to the station on N. Larrabee St. Arriving at 8:15 AM, Elaina and Henrique Sanchez were already at work and Morgan Latner soon followed. We huddled for around 20 minutes on the judge Eggleston murder. They did find a 22 caliber shell casing this time, but no other physical evidence. Their plan was to check in on the judge's wife and then go back to further canvass the neighborhood.

Detective Rodriguez and I would go over to the car impound lot around 9 AM to meet up with the CSI team and thoroughly inspect

Cheryl Greenberg's car. As our meeting was breaking up, a call came in for me from Special Agent Teresa Marek. She explained that there were some new developments in their investigation of the white supremacist group, First Patriots, and their connection to the Russian mob in Chicago. They wanted to meet with us right away. I told her that Detective Rodriguez and I would be at their office after searching Greenberg's car.

At the impound lot the CSI crew headed by Sgt. Tom Sprague was just getting started. They began by dusting the outside of the Lexus for fingerprints and looking for any kind of hair, fiber or other DNA. The same procedure was repeated on the inside including vacuuming the floor mats and between and under the seats.

When they were finished, I asked Sgt. Sprague for a pair of his surgical gloves and leaned into the passenger side. I bent down and looked under the seat and reached my arm all the way under, sweeping and feeling the underside. There was nothing. I went around to the driver side and reached under the seat and felt nothing unusual until I move my hand up and felt something very different than I felt on the passenger side. It was a hard smooth surface with some kind of indentation in the center of it. I continued feeling around its surface until I found an edge and gently put some pressure on it until it slowly came off emitting the unmistakable sound of Velcro.

Standing up, I raised up a silver Hewlett-Packard laptop. Elaina said something in Spanish that I took for meaning bravo! I thanked the CSI team and informed Sgt. Sprague that we would be taking the laptop and would check it into the evidence room later. I also asked him to keep it to himself. Especially, if detectives from the carjacking task force came by asking questions.

"Are you thinking what I'm thinking?" Elaina said with a sly grin. "What you are holding in your hands Jack, is pure dynamite. There are a lot of dangerous people looking for that thing."

"Yeah, we're on the same page Elaina." I responded. I'm going to put this in my car and take it home with me tonight. It should be safe in the station parking lot for today. Let's pay a visit to Agents Marek and Wright. I'm anxious to hear about the new developments.

After a quick stop at my Camaro, we drove directly to FBI headquarters and within 20 minutes Elaina was pulling our gray Impala into the parking lot of the FBI building on W. Roosevelt Rd. We passed through security and then up to the office where Agents Teresa Marek and Tony Wright were waiting for us.

We exchanged brief greetings, and Tony Wright asked us to sit down and got up to close the office door. "The timing of your visit is very fortuitous." He started. "There has been quite a bit of chatter picked up between the First Patriots group and elements of the Russian mob in Chicago. That in and of itself is not surprising, but we've also picked up communications between the supremacist movement and known members of organized crime groups in the Deep South, commonly referred to as the Dixie Mafia. This is something new to us, and we're not sure what to make of it right now."

"Have you been able to determine the purpose of their communications?" Elaina asked.

Teresa Marek answered. "Not exactly, but there have been references to the delivery of commodities and also large-scale shipping. We aren't sure who the exact players are, but the calls from the South have been originating in Mississippi and going to untraceable mobile phones moving around the North and Northwest Sides of Chicago. We think that the commodities they are talking about, could be stolen cars or car parts."

"Have you been able to figure out how some of the vehicles that are equipped with tracking devices are being tracked into the Ukrainian Village area and then they go ghost?" I inquired.

"We have a theory." Wright responded. "It is likely that the vehicles are driven into any one of several of the many gas stations or garages in that area. They are quickly able to remove the GPS devices or somehow disable the built in systems. We're not sure exactly how they're doing it, but we have our technical people working on it."

"We have had that experience recently. We were right on a stolen car in Ukrainian Village and were closing in, but then, all of a sudden, we lost the signal. We checked out several gas stations and garages in the immediate area, but couldn't find anything." I said.

"Yes, this has been a pattern." Marek added. "We don't think the cars stay in the Ukrainian Village, though. The facilities in that neighborhood are large enough to house the growing number of vehicles being taken. And it is worth noting that in other parts of the city the majority of stolen cars are recovered in one form or another. But, not on the North Side. During the past six months only 10% of the stolen vehicles have been recovered there."

"Have you turned up anything on the detectives in the carjacking unit like Anderson, Solar, O'Brien and Nijinsky or any of the others?" I asked changing the subject.

Agent Wright replied. "We are working on it. But we do have something that we have decided to share with you."

"We have had an agent within the First Patriot group for a couple of months now, Teresa Marek continued." He is considered a newbie and only has access to limited information about their up activities. They are a crude bunch, but very cautious and street smart. He has been given some superficial duties related to recruiting and fundraising, but he is trying to slowly gain their trust. We will keep you informed. Obviously, you both realize how sensitive this information is."

Elaina and I nodded. "We have learned to be cautious about sharing information. We are keeping some things to ourselves at the moment in relation to the Cheryl Greenberg murder. We will let you know if we get anything worthwhile out of it."

We all got up shook hands and promised to stay in touch. They had given us a lot to think about, and now it was our job to tie it all together with the murders on our plate.

On the way back to the station we decided to stop somewhere for lunch, and driving east on Roosevelt Rd., Elaina turned left on

S. Halsted St. "I haven't been to Greektown in a while. How about the Athena?", Elaina suggested.

"Sounds good to me." I answered enthusiastically. "I love Greektown, and I haven't been to the Athena yet."

Only a few blocks up Halsted St., Elaina took a parking space almost directly across from the restaurant. We crossed the busy road and entered the front door of the classic Greek styled establishment. A young woman approached us and Elaina asked for a table outside. She walked us through the ornate main dining room filled with covered tables, a bright blue and white chandelier, light blue walls, a fireplace and panels of bright blue stained glass and out into a much less formal garden dining area.

We were seated at a nice sized garden table. The area was surrounded by high vine covered walls and flower beds. The soft September air created the feeling of experiencing a Mediterranean feast. When our server, a tall slender middle-aged man with short salt-and-pepper hair, arrived, we ordered iced teas and appetizers of Saganaki pan-fried cheese and Greek salads. Elaina chose a main course of the combination platter which included leg of lamb, rice and potato. I went for the Athenian chicken in lemon and white wine with rice and potato.

Our conversation turned to what we had learned from our FBI partners. We both felt that the carjacking activities in the Near North and other Northside neighborhoods were connected to the murder of Cheryl Greenberg and the witness, Jay Farrell as well as threats being made toward us and other people in the legal system and now the murder of Judge John Eggleston in the Gold Coast.

The carjackings and thefts were on a large scale which indicated an organized business motivated by making large profits. But the threats and murder of a Circuit Court Judge indicated the actions of a radical hate group. Can they be working together?

That thought lingered, as our Saganaki and salads were delivered, and our appetites overpowered our curiosity for the next 30 minutes including our enjoyment of delicious main dishes in such pleasant September surroundings.

Then the mood took a dark turn. My phone sounded with notification of an incoming text. I open my phone and read a crude and threatening message. It referred to my father and all the n..... loving defense lawyers. It threatened me, Elaina and anyone in the legal system who didn't follow their rules. It went on, "we can take out anybody we want. No judge, cop or lawyer is now safe. And we can take you any time Fallon. The FBI won't save you. We're ready for them too."

I looked at a Elaina and told her that the text was from the First Patriot scumbags. Then I responded. "Why don't we get together. I would really like to see a first-class ass hole face-to-face."

"Your time will come detective. And it could happen sooner than you think."

An uneasy feeling in my stomach replaced the satisfying fullness of our sumptuous meal. "I've got a hunch, partner, and I need to act on it right now. I'm going to go out the back here and check the Street. Keep texting the freak on the other end using the term ass hole every once in a while. No Spanish insults. Okay?"

"Si compadre." She responded, as I stood up and handed her my phone.

"Walk out the front door in about 10 minutes. Looks like you're picking up the check on this one, partner."

I surveyed the garden area and spotted an exit on the back left corner of the courtyard. It opened to an alley which ran parallel to Halsted Street. I decided to go right heading north to the end of the block which left me around 40 yards away from our gray Impala parked on the other side of the street.

The alley was quiet, and it was a short walk to Hallstead which was experiencing moderate early afternoon traffic. A few pedestrians were coming in and out of the restaurants and shops, and nothing suspicious caught my eye, until I crossed the street and got about 30 feet from our car. Then I noticed two things at the same time that put me on high alert.

I could clearly see two legs sticking out from under the front end of our Impala. Two parked cars beyond that, I recognized the silver Ford F150 and a shadowy figure in the driver seat wearing a black hoodie and sunglasses. My heart rate increased along with my pace.

When I got closer, the guy in the F150 hit the horn and a stocky guy with dark brown shaggy hair dressed in an auto mechanics gray shirt and pants scrambled out from under the front end of our car and hopped up looking alarmed.

As soon as he spotted me, he turned and tried to run toward the silver truck, but I tackled him, and we went down onto the sidewalk. He was strong, and I had a hard time controlling him to get cuffs on him. I heard the truck door slam shut and feared that the driver would soon be on me. So, I grabbed my guy by his hair and slammed his face down on the sidewalk until he went limp.

I popped up just in time to see that the hooded guy was about 5 feet away from me. He pulled a revolver out of his belt and took a step close enough to me that I kicked his right wrist, and the gun went flying. The tall slender assailant looked all too familiar. This was definitely the guy at the Baha'i Temple service and probably the guy in the Ford F150 at my dad's barbecue. My blood was boiling.

He pulled a switchblade out of his boot and opened it while lunging at me. I stepped to my left and his thrust with his right hand caught my right side enough that I felt the knife slice through the outer flesh. I grabbed his wrist and turned the knife in toward him and plunged it into his right thigh. He howled in pain and blood began gushing out of his leg.

Before I could fully subdue this guy, I got spun around and realized that the first guy was back at me, and he got me off balance causing me to have to grab onto him and pull him down hard. This time I got on top of him and noticed that he was bleeding profusely from his nose and he had lost some of his strength. I turned him and quickly got cuffs on him and turned my attention back to the hoodie.

He was seriously injured but was able to limp to his truck and managed to get in. He got it started and began pulling out into the street. At that time, I spotted a cell phone in his hand and Elaina coming out of the Athena and beginning to cross Hallsted heading toward our car.

I yelled to her at the top of my lungs to stop and go back. She halted and I yelled again and just as she turned her back there was a thunderous boom and our car exploded, sending a huge ball of fire toward the sky and plumes of gray and black smoke in every direction.

The silver Ford truck zoomed down the smoke shrouded Street. And, I ran into the thick dark clouds, desperately seeking my partner.

Chapter 16

I ran into the murky dark haze, but quickly slowed down because the visibility was almost zero. In a matter of moments, I began tripping and nearly went down. Looking back I saw the outline of a figure sitting upright on the pavement next to the curb. Then the figure spoke.

"Take it easy Jack. I already feel like I've been kicked by a horse. Help me up."

I grabbed Elaina's forearms when she reached out to me and guided her to her feet. The sharp pain in my right side made me wince, but the intense heat I felt on my back instantly directed my focus to something more immediately dangerous.

I grabbed my partner around the waist and told her to move her butt right now! "That gas tank hasn't blown yet!" We hustled through the smoke toward where I estimated the entrance to the Athena was located. We literally bumped into the front windows of the restaurant and felt our way, until we got to the front door. I was relieved to find it intact and unlocked. We rushed in and continued toward the back as stunned patrons and staff looked on. And then, just as I was telling everybody to get into the courtyard, there was a second huge explosion causing the building to shake and one of the front windows to shatter.

Outside smoke and fire rose up from what was left of our in Impala, and the sounds of screams and gasps were giving way to the blaring siren sounds of multiple emergency vehicles. There was no way of knowing whether other vehicles were now on fire and in danger of exploding. So, Elaina and I continued to shepherd the crowd out into the back courtyard.

Finally, after everyone was away from the devastation on Halsted Street, I had a chance to check on Elaina after I got her to sit down at one of the outside tables. "Are you hurt? Did you get hit with anything?"

She hesitated before responding. "I don't think so. I didn't see it coming. I didn't know anything was going on. I was still looking at your phone when the damn bomb went off." Then she raised her right hand and started laughing. It was still holding my phone.

I couldn't help laughing myself, as she reached out and handed it to me. "Great plan Jack. You could have at least told me what you were up to. I could have skipped paying the bill. "We both laughed again, and this time the pain in my side caused me to swear in protest, and Elaina told me to sit down.

"Jack you're bleeding a lot. Here take my chair. Go on, sit down right now!" She grabbed a clean cloth table napkin and pressed it into my side after lifting up my ripped shirt and exposing a long gash in my side. After pulling up a chair to sit beside me, she called for an ambulance and reported that we were on the scene in the Athena courtyard.

Before long police officers and firemen began streaming into the courtyard and directing people out the back way and asking for any injured people to remain sitting. Almost everyone exited into the alley. When they got to us, Elaina informed them about the knife wound to my right side, and I asked them to check my partner out for possible concussion symptoms.

The EMTs that arrived did their work masterfully by treating my wound with antibacterial ointment and bandage wrapped my waist and by checking Elaina's eyes and asking her some basic questions. They told us that we were both going to be taken by ambulance to Northwestern Memorial Hospital, but before we got up to leave, two detectives showed up.

It was Detectives Beth Howard and Nick Salerno from the Near West District. I was familiar with Beth from my days on patrol in Austin, and Elaina knew Nick. So, we exchanged greetings, and I filled them in on what had gone down and some of the background concerning the threats made to us and others and the possible connection to carjackings in the city.

"That's interesting." Beth Howard interjected. "No wonder we've got carjacking task force detectives all over the place out there."

Elaina and I couldn't help looking at each other and smirking. "Yeah we've had contact with some of them ourselves. Are you guys familiar with any of them? "I asked.

Nick Salerno spoke up. "I know Roger O'Brien and have met his partner Carl Nijinsky and a couple other detectives on their task force. But, there are a couple of real beauties out there that we don't know. Right Beth?"

"Yeah." Beth responded. "The two guys Anderson and Solar are out there trying to run the show. We may have to straighten them out."

"We have had some pleasant experiences with those two. Have fun with that." Elaina said with a laugh.

"We'll be sure to give them a nice Near West welcome." Nick said smiling. Then the EMTs cut the conversation short and whisked both of us off to Northwestern Memorial.

When we arrived at the emergency room, Elaina and I were taken in different directions for intake and examinations by different physicians. I was first treated by nurse Abby Fowler and then Dr. Ronald Weiland. The good doctor informed me that I was fortunate that my wound wasn't too deep but at 5 inches long it required 30 stitches and a prescription for antibiotics.

I was discharged around two hours later and saw my partner sitting in the waiting room. She had been released a few minutes earlier. They determined that although she didn't have a severe concussion, she was instructed to stay out of work for a few days and avoid any strenuous exercise. And, since I was given the same marching orders, we decided to report back to Lieut. Whitehead at the station and take it from there.

I called dispatch for a ride and within 15 minutes we were walking into our headquarters. We went directly to Tyrone Whitehead's office and walked through the open door.

The Lieutenant waved us in and asked us to sit down. He was aware in general of the car bombing incident, but wanted to hear about it from us. Elaina nodded to me, and I proceeded to tell the story, beginning with our meeting at the FBI building and culminating with my confrontation with the two jagoffs on Halsted Street after receiving the threats and just before the car bomb was detonated.

Whitehead had sat quietly listening intently, until I was finished. He informed us that he was aware of some developments that the FBI was concerned about on a national scale, and that seemed to be manifesting themselves in Chicago at that time. He believed that our homicide investigations and the big increase in Northside carjackings were related and wanted us to continue cooperating with Special Agents Marek and Wright.

The Lieutenant ordered us to take the weekend off and follow doctor's orders. He also stated that he was adding Detectives Zileen Baker and George Makris to our team. "You two can communicate with your team from home. Try to take it easy this weekend, but whatever you do don't take the threats lightly."

We went to the detectives' room and held a short conference with our team of detectives who all happened to be present. Baker and Makris were brought up to speed, as much as was needed at the moment, and it was decided that they and Detectives Latner and Sanchez would focus on the murder of Judge Eggleston and follow-up with Detectives Beth Howard and Nick Salerno from the Near West on any connection between the bombing and carjackings in the Near North.

Elaina and I parted ways in the station parking lot, and I gingerly climbed into my Camaro without knowing where I was going. Pulling out of the lot instead of turning left on N. Larrabee St. to go home, I went right towards downtown and my father's office in the George W. Dunne Cook County Office Building on W. Washington St. Something was telling me to check in on my dad.

After a short ride, I used the self parking garage on N. Dearborn St. and made the easy walk to the classic international style concrete behemoth befitting Chicago's image of being the city with the broad shoulders. Built in 1965 it has floor to ceiling windows on the cavernous archway filled first floor and is connected to an underground pedestrian ped way that makes dozens of buildings as well as the subway easily accessible on the many days of Chicago's inclement weather.

Walking into the building, I greeted the security guards, some of whom recognized me and waved me through. I went to the familiar bank of elevators servicing the 37 floors and pushed a button for one going to the public defender's office on the 17th floor.

Exiting the elevator, the Public Defender's Office was immediately to the right, and I entered it, as I had done many times before, beginning with trips accompanying my father to work as a child. Those visits usually occurred on Saturdays and were a source of excitement and pride to a young boy who found it hard to believe that his dad worked in such a fantastical place.

The longtime receptionist, Leslie Lupo, greeted me and scolded me playfully for not visiting in such a long time. I apologized profusely, and we chatted for a few minutes, before she released me to my father. I walked down the bustling corridor of offices containing a small army of hard charging defense attorneys.

I couldn't help thinking that so few people realize how hard the lawyers in the criminal justice system work. The detectives and police officers naturally were more familiar with the caseload of the prosecutor's at the States Attorney's Office, but I also knew the other side of it, having grown up watching my dad and his fellow public defender's working late nights and weekends for clients who so often either had no appreciation or were downright hostile toward them.

His office door was always open, and I breezed right in, and as usual he was busy typing on the keyboard and staring intently at the desktop screen. Without looking, he just asked his unknown visitor to give him a second and continued typing.

After waiting a couple of minutes I decided to break his concentration. "Whatever he's charged with, I'm sure he's guilty."

That did it. His face at first showed a furled brow and curled lip which soon turned into a wide smile.

He popped out of his chair and quickly moved around his desk and moved in for his usual embrace. I had to literally give him a stiff arm placing my left hand on his chest. "Sorry dad. I am a little sore on my right side."

"Oh I'm sorry. What the hell happened Jack?"

I spent the next few minutes relating what happened in Greektown and assuring him that I would be fine, and that Elaina was okay too. He had always been unflappable at home and in the courtroom, but this time he couldn't disguise the look of concern on his face. He uncharacteristically closed the office door and walked back around the desk and motioned for me to sit down.

"Dad, I wanted to come down here to see you because I'm worried about you. There's so much crazy shit going on that I don't know what to expect next. Threats are going out in all directions to people involved in the criminal justice system. Have you had any more threats here?"

My father nodded. "Yeah we've had a lot of them in just the last couple of days. They threatened the Public Defender's Office in general, but many are directed specifically at me and Linda Prassas. You know, it is weird. Whoever is making the threats seems to be just as focused on the Billy Sims case which we lost, as they are on cases that we won. It just doesn't make sense."

"I know dad. There was something about the Sims case that really stinks. I was in the courtroom when Sims attacked Terrance Goggins. Something about it just wasn't right. I know what Sims claims Goggins said, but I couldn't hear or see anything from where I was sitting."

"Yeah Jack, since Linda Prassas put in her notice of appeal this morning, the threats really intensified. And the weird thing is that the notice doesn't state what the basis of the appeal will be. And yet, the threats mention lies about prosecutorial misconduct coming from our office and others."

"I think I may know something about that, but there are some things going on that I can't discuss with you right now. It's getting more complicated every day. I'm very worried about you dad. I wish you could go someplace for a while. Maybe go stay with Molly in Evanston or get a hotel room."

"You know I can't do that, son. I would never put Molly at risk, and a hotel isn't practical. How long am I supposed to do that? No. We all take risks in this business. We'll get through this. You take care of yourself. Promise me."

"I will. I promise." Getting up slowly, I moved around my father's desk and gave him a long warm hug. Let the pain be damned.

Chapter 17

My next stop was just three floors up at the State's Attorney's offices on the 20th floor. Upon walking through the main entrance, I was once again greeted by a familiar face. The receptionist, Emily Foley. "Hi there, Jack. Haven't seen you in a while. Do you have an appointment with someone, or is this a social call? I understand that you have a new friend in the Major Crimes Division."

I couldn't help noticing the twinkle in the eyes of the attractive young receptionist with long brown hair. Her sly smile made me laugh. "You got me Emily. I confess. I guess good news travels fast too. Is Paige available?"

"Let me check. I know they are preparing for a meeting with some detectives from the carjacking task force. Why don't you take a seat, and I'll go back and check on it."

I sat down in the waiting area on a three seater black leather couch. The office was a bustling place just like the Public Defender's Office had been, and like every police station in the city is. Attorneys came in and out as well as some State's Attorney's investigators. No one paid much attention to me except one of the investigators, Dan Phillips who I was familiar with. He just said hi and kept on about his business. Everyone there was used to seeing officers and detectives on a regular basis. In theory we were all on the same team.

Soon Emily Foley reappeared and informed me that Attorney Owira would be right out. She went back to her desk laughing. "Not even any flowers or a gift for her birthday?"

I jumped to my feet and the pain in my side shot through me like a long hot needle. "You're kidding me right!", I exclaimed. "I had no idea!"

"Relax Jack. Sit back down. You look like you're in pain. Yeah, I was kidding. I got you good though, didn't I? But I think she's really got you."

Before I could respond appropriately, Paige walked into the reception area as our eyes locked into one another's. She kept a straight face, and I did my best to do the same."Nice to see you Detective Fallon. You must be here for the carjacking meeting. You're a little early, but why don't you come down to the conference room with me."

I followed her down the long hallway filled with prosecutors still at their desks working to finish up as much as possible even though it was a Friday afternoon after 5 PM. She led me into a nice sized conference room and shut the door before moving quickly into a warm close embrace.

I eagerly engaged in her sensual and arousing hug, until the pain in my side caused me to reluctantly disentangle myself from her amorous embrace. I explained to her the cause of my need to step back from her, and she immediately became concerned and apologetic.

I assured her that I was fine and appreciative of the hug. But before I could tell her anymore about it, the conference room door opened, and in walked a middle-aged woman and a young man both dressed like lawyers.

Paige introduced them as Assistant State's Attorneys Tara Thistle and Jason Smith. We shook hands all around, and Tara took the floor. "Are you here for the task force briefing Detective Fallon? I don't have you on my list, but you are welcome to join in."

The way Paige looked at me made my decision easy. "Sure. I would be happy to sit in on the briefing. As you probably know, I am in Homicide in the Near North, but some of our cases have direct or indirect connections to carjackings."

At that there was a knock on the open door and Emily Foley announced that the task force detectives had arrived. Attorney Thistle asked her to show them in and away she went.

A minute later we could hear the sounds of footsteps on the tiled floor in the hallway. The first to enter were the familiar faces of Detectives Roger O'Brien and Carl Nijinsky followed by two unfamiliar ones and then the familiar but unpleasant faces of Oscar Anderson and Jorge Solar.

Tara Thistle again took the lead in introducing everyone, as she acknowledged that some of us may already know each other. O'Brien and Nijinsky greeted me, and Anderson and Solar just mumbled something while the two new detectives, Stan Weber and Nina Del Bacaro, offered handshakes and greetings.

Attorney Thistle asked us all to sit down and then explained that she had invited me to attend the meeting since I happened to stop by, and she was aware that I was working on some cases that may be both carjacking and homicide related. She hoped no one would object.

Four of the detectives expressed that they were either happy to have my participation, or that they had no objection. Detective Solar just sat there scowling, and Detective Anderson shrugged and said that while he didn't think it was necessary, he wouldn't object.

From there Tara Thistle began the meeting by discussing the specific charges against a couple of defendants who were in custody and awaiting trial on carjacking and other related crimes. Detectives O'Brien and Nijinsky were set to testify along with Weber and Del Bacaro in one case and were involved in the second case, in which Detectives Anderson and Solar were scheduled to testify.

Attorney Thistle went on to detail the timetables for various hearings mostly involving what evidence would be allowed to be presented at trial. She also discussed which of the attorneys on their team would be handling each specific hearing. Paige was assigned several of them, and she discussed procedure and scheduled meetings with whichever detectives were involved.

After the trial preparations were fully laid out for the detectives, attorney Thistle turned the discussion to taking a more general big picture look at the carjacking problem and the recent surge taking place on the North Side of Chicago

Detective O'Brien reported on the rising numbers of carjackings and stolen vehicles in general in the Near North neighborhood as well as others along Lake Michigan including Lincoln Park, Lakeview and all the way up to Rogers Park.

Anderson and Solar revealed their figures from North Side central neighborhoods such as Avondale, Logan Square, Wicker Park, and Ukrainian Village among others. While Detectives Weber and Del Bacaro focused on the Northwest Side neighborhoods such as Irving Park, Dunning, Portage Park and Montclare.

All three sectors were seeing significant increases in overall vehicle thefts and carjackings with a few exceptions on the far Northwest Side. The issue of violence connected to the stolen autos was also seen to be on the rise and troubling.

Near the end of the meeting, Oscar Anderson turned his attention to me and what he saw as a lack of cooperation from Near North detectives and especially myself and partner Elaina Rodriguez. He specifically pointed to the Cheryl Greenberg murder and his belief that we were withholding evidence from the carjacking task force.

I looked hard at Detective Anderson and responded. "We have been and will continue to cooperate with our fellow detectives from the task force, but we will not turn over a homicide investigation in our district to any outside detectives. And the last time I looked, homicide takes precedence over car theft."

This seemed to get a rise out of Detectives Anderson and Solar who unsurprisingly objected to my characterization of our interactions. They both stood up and leaned across the conference table threateningly toward me. When I stood up, Solar took a swing at me which I ducked and in the same motion pulled his tie hard jerking his head face first down onto the hard surface. Anderson leapt over the table and grabbed my shoulders but couldn't hold on, and I threw him off and sent him sprawling onto the floor.

The attorneys sat stunned at the chaotic scene as Detectives O'Brien and Weber jumped in and blocked Anderson and Solar from engaging with me again. Anderson was enraged and Detective

Nijinsky assisted O'Brien in subduing him, but Solar was bleeding profusely from his nose and had lost his steam.

I didn't even notice that Attorney Thistle had slipped out of the conference room and returned with several State's Attorney's investigators who quickly escorted Anderson and Solar out of the room and down the hall. I looked over at Paige who was clearly shaken and tried to give her assurance with a smile and then turned my attention to the others. "I am sorry about that guys, but my partner and I have had trouble with those two before. I don't know what their problem is."

"Don't worry about it Fallon." Detective O'Brien said as Nijinsky nodded. "Nobody in the task force gets along with those guys. Feel free to contact Nijinsky and me. We will be happy to share information and work with you and Rodriguez. Detectives Del Bacaro and Weber seconded that sentiment and Tara Thistle thanked all of us for participating in the meeting.

As we all started to leave the conference room, attorney Thistle called me back. "Detective Fallon would you mind staying for a minute? I need to have a word with you and Attorney Owira. Attorney Smith will you excuse us please."

As soon as Jason Smith exited the room, she closed the door behind him and asked us to sit down. "Jack I wanted to let you know that we are taking the threats made toward Paige very seriously. Being a detective, I'm sure that you understand that some animosity and level of threat comes with the territory in our line of work. But, for a threatening letter to be left on Paige's desk is alarming. It is unfortunate, but we are considering tighter security measures here. I understand that Paige is staying with you for the time being."

"That's right. She will be staying with me, for as long as we feel it is necessary, and for as long as she wants." The smile on Paige's face made me realize how far and fast our relationship had come in just a few days, and I wasn't fighting it.

"I think that is a great idea. With all the crazy things happening out there right now, we can't be too careful. The Judge Eggleston murder is off the charts, and I heard about what happened in Greektown today. Are you okay?"

"Yeah, it only hurts when I laugh or breathe." I responded while laughing and wincing. But I am still worried about what has been going on right here at the State's Attorney's Office and especially with the homicide prosecutors like Terrance Goggins. Do you think they could be responsible for the threats?"

"Well, I'd hate to think so." Tara responded ."They are kind of an aggressive group of lawyers and some of them are sort of wound up over the Sims cases, especially since Attorney Linda Prassas put in her notice of appeal. The rumor is that she is going to pursue a claim of prosecutorial misconduct. So, that has gotten Goggins and others riled up. Still, I wouldn't expect any of them to cross the line with threats or actions.

"I hope you're right." I said, and Paige nodded in agreement." I feel safe here with Tara and Jason's help. And, of course with you Jack." She reached out and touched my hand sending a charge of electricity through my body, as Tara Thistle looked on smiling.

"Go ahead Paige. Get out of here. It's Friday night. Have some fun and take care of Detective Fallon. Don't worry about coming in tomorrow. I'll see you Monday morning, and feel free to call if you need anything. I don't live too far from you in Noble Square."

Paige gathered up her things including her briefcase and laptop. We walked to her car parked nearby and agreed to meet at the parking area at the Covington Apartments, as soon as we could get there.

Around 20 minutes later I pulled my Camaro into the Covington and found Paige already waiting in one of the guest spots nearby. I motioned for her to join me, and she came over and climbed into the passenger side. "Let's go to the grocery store and get enough supplies for the weekend. I'm supposed to lay low for a few days. Doctor's orders. So, we might as well have plenty of good food on hand."

We stopped by the Old World Market on North Broadway, and Paige took over. She filled our cart with a wide variety of items and ingredients enough for several sumptuous meals. I added a 12 pack of Miller High Life and a couple of bottles of wine, and we headed back to my apartment to spend a quiet and hopefully uneventful weekend.

Chapter 18

Monday morning came too soon for both of us. Except for a short walk in the park on Sunday afternoon, we spent the whole weekend in my apartment feasting on amazing meals prepared entirely by Paige. She wouldn't let me do anything because of my injury. I was totally pampered and loved it.

As it turns out, Paige learned all about Southern cooking from her Alabama born and bred mother and knew how to make delicious Japanese dishes from her father. I enjoyed cooking, but my skills didn't compare to hers, and it was really nice being with someone again.

We were up early, and the sun was shining through the east facing living room windows. It was going to be a warm September day that was still whispering of summer. After a light breakfast we were dressed and ready for work. It was clear to me that she took her job as seriously as I did, and even with everything that was going on, she remained focused on her cases.

We agreed to get in touch later in the day and drove out of the Covington toward Lakeshore Drive. I tried to keep her in front of me but soon lost her in the heavy morning traffic. After that happened, my mind turned entirely to what needed to be done that day. I arrived at the station at 8:05 AM and only Zileen Baker was in ahead of me. But by 8:20 AM the rest of the team had arrived.

When everyone had (+had?) a chance to get some coffee and open up their desktops, I called us together and laid out the day's plan of attack. Detectives Morgan Latner and Henrique Sanchez would continue working on Judge John Eggleston's murder by canvassing the Gold Coast neighborhood looking for witnesses and cameras. Detectives Zileen Baker and George Makris would focus on the killing of witness Jay Farrell as well as the attack on Rachel Braun and Elaina, and I would follow the leads we had in the Cheryl

Greenberg case. None of us had received any new threats over the weekend, but we all agreed to remain super vigilant, nonetheless.

Elaina and I knew that the first thing on our list was to drive up to the Michigan Shores Club in Wilmette to meet Cheryl Greenberg's longtime friend Patti Vail. We were hoping she could either give us the password to Greenberg's laptop or help us figure it out.

We were assigned a black Chevy Malibu and Elaina was driving us north on Lakeshore Drive by 9 AM. The traffic going out of town wasn't too bad. On the way up to the North Shore we caught up on how our weekends went and any new thoughts about the cases, we were working on, as well as how they were connected to carjackings and our car bombing.

Elaina felt that all of it was connected somehow, but the hard part was the how and why. The carjackings seemed to be organized and done for profit since so many of the vehicles stolen on the North Side in recent months had not been recovered, unlike what was going on in the rest of the city. But, the murders and threats seemed to be personal and motivated by some kind of radical agenda.

I agreed and expressed that I thought Victor Kirilenko could be the key. He was a Russian immigrant living in Ukrainian Village involved with carjackings and the Russian mob. According to Cheryl Greenberg's partner Matt Giordano he was about to cooperate and had some bombshell information to share. It seemed that whatever it was got him killed. We needed to get into that damn laptop.

Elaina parked the Malibu on Michigan Avenue right in front of the stately stone Tudor structure on the shores of Lake Michigan. The soft September morning elevated the feeling of serene tranquility. We were only 20 miles from the loop, but it seemed a world away.

Inside, the lobby was calm and quiet. Margaret was smiling and waving at us from behind the reception desk. We returned her greeting and got right to the point. Looking toward the windows facing the pool, I asked if we could speak with Patti Vail.

"Oh my." Margaret responded. "I completely forgot to mention this whole thing to Patti, when she called this morning."

"Did she call in sick today?" Elaina asked ."We can go to her. This is very important. Where does she live?"

"Well, she lives nearby in Evanston. But she isn't there. She and her boyfriend are having such a nice time in this wonderful weather up in Wisconsin they decided to stay a little longer. They're coming back tomorrow night. She'll be back to work here Wednesday morning."

"What's the cell number? We need to talk to her today!" I exclaimed urgently

"I can give you her cell number, but she doesn't get reception up there. She called from a little grocery store in some tiny town. Besides, she likes to turn her phone off, when she goes camping. You know, to really get away."

"Yeah we know. Must be nice. It's not something we have the luxury of experiencing." Elaina commented.

I could tell by the expression on Margaret's face that she thought that was too bad. She gave us the cell phone number and promised to try to remember to tell Patti that we wanted to talk to her if she called again.

"Man, that really sucks!" I belted out as soon as we got outside." Let's not waste the trip up here. We could go up to Glencoe and check in with Capt. Norris."

Elaina liked the idea, and we once again took Sheridan Road on the scenic drive to Glencoe. Turning left on Park Avenue, we drove past the Greenberg's residence on the way to the Glencoe Police Department. This time we were in luck, and the man we needed to see was at work. The desk officer called him, and then walked us down a short hallway and showed us into the captain's modest but well- appointed office.

"You have good timing detectives," the large imposing police Captain said. "There was a break in at the Greenberg's last evening, while they were out to dinner. We were there all night processing the scene. Our CSI people just left about an hour ago."

"Whoa. Do you think it is related to our case Captain? I mean Cheryl's murder."

"Yeah. We think so. They ransacked the whole house this time ripping up the couches, chairs and mattresses even the car seats in the Mercedes that was in their garage. But, as far as the Greenberg's can tell, they didn't take anything. This certainly wasn't a typical North Shore burglary."

"The same thing happened at Greenberg's law office." I responded." There looking for some specific items relating to something much bigger that Cheryl was working on. I don't think they will come back to Glencoe. At this point they should be convinced that what they are after isn't up here. But, please let us know of any developments."

We walked out to our car and decided to go directly back to the reality of the harsher but more enriching world we experienced living in the great city of Chicago. The North Shore life was a great thing I thought. But it wasn't mine, and I didn't mind it at all.

I suggested that we check in with the Near West detectives that responded to our car bombing crime scene, and Elaina agreed. I had Detective Beth Howard's number in my phone and called her as we left Sheridan Road and entered Lakeshore Drive heading south.

Beth Howard answered right away and said that she and her partner Nick Salerno were just about to call us. They were leaving their station to interview the defendant that I had tangled with on Halsted Street just before the explosion. He was at the Cook County Jail, and she invited us to join them. I readily accepted. So, we were now on our way down to 26th and California to the monstrosity of a city jail housing approximately 7500 inmates.

When we arrived at the imposing prison facility, Detectives Salerno and Howard informed us that the defendant had been identified as a 37-year-old career criminal named Oren Clanton. He had convictions for armed robbery and Grand Theft Auto in

Alabama and Mississippi and was known to have ties to organized crime in Mobile and Biloxi.

After passing through a series of locked steel doors and walking several long hallways, we arrived at the division 10 men's maximum-security pod. Guards placed in a secure observation post in the center of the large common area buzzed the door, and our jail guard escort lead us into one of Cook County jail's most dangerous places to be.

The guard directed us to a locked conference room, and another steel door buzzed. Our escort opened it and waved us inside, where there were a couple of chairs and a thick Plexiglas window dividing the room. On the other side of it sat Oren Clanton, the guy who had attempted to kill Elaina and me and who took a good beating in the process.

Clanton stared at us defiantly which I might have found to be humorous, since he had a butterfly bandage on his nose and was sporting two colorful black eyes, if the circumstances weren't so serious. Detectives Salerno and Howard had already read him his Miranda rights and obtained his signature to that affect, so the usual preliminary discourse wasn't necessary.

Howard and Salerno took the chairs next to the glass and the small voice portal. Before they could ask any questions, Clanton smiled and started a rambling vulgar diatribe directed at us and the legal community in general. I couldn't help laughing at his ignorant bravado which really seemed to set him off.

"You may laugh now Detective Fallon, but we're going to wipe that smile off your face. We're going to wipe out all of you and your illegitimate government traitors."

"Big words from a little man." I countered. "Just how do you intend to accomplish all of this Oren? Sounds like you have big plans. You're going to need a lot of help to pull something like this off. I think you're full of BS. You and your little band of car thieves don't have the smarts or the resources to do anything important."

My words produced the intended result. Clanton became enraged and jumped to his feet sputtering an angry threatening response. "We are much bigger than you ever dreamed of, and soon were going to have everything we need to bring the fight to your doorstep. You are all going down. Every one of you participating in your so-called legal system will be wiped out along with your families, until we the real Americans are in control of everything. It's coming hard and it's coming soon!"

At that, there was a knock at the door and the guard opened it and in walked a short slender white guy looking to be around 40 years old and dressed in a tan three-piece suit. He wore steel framed rectangular shaped glasses and spoke in a soft almost effeminate voice creating a stark contrast with the growling testosterone overloaded presence of his client, Mr. Oren Clanton.

"Excuse me ladies and gentlemen, my name is Shelby Warren Gately the third. And I must kindly ask you to immediately leave so that I may have a confidential consultation with my client. Please do not contact Mr. Clanton again without my presence and consent." Attorney Gately announced before handing each of us his card which showed a phone number, fax, email and an address in Mobile Alabama.

We all filed out of the conference room and followed our escort on the security door filled procession while exiting the cavernous Cook County Jail. No one said anything, until we had collected our firearms and stepped out onto the sidewalk and breathed what seemed to be the freshest air I had experienced in a very long time. It was always a good feeling upon leaving a jail, but after being in the same room with a vile creature like Oren Clanton the warm September breeze felt and smelled even sweeter.

"Well, that didn't get us anywhere." Nick Salerno noted. "Sorry we brought you down here for this waste of time. But I think the State's Attorney's Office has enough to move forward with Clanton's prosecution. We will keep working on tracing the bomb components and identifying whoever has had contact with this asshole. We'll keep you guys in the loop."

"We appreciate that." Elaina responded. "I'm sure that the State's Attorney's Office will be getting in touch with us too. After all, we were the victims and witnesses."

Once in the car I shared my impression of our meeting with Oren Clanton. "I'm not so sure that was all a waste of time Elaina. Somewhere in that unhinged rant of his there may be some useful information. If they are planning something on a much larger scale that is imminent, our FBI friends may be interested in hearing about our little chat with our car bomber."

Elaina drove north on California Avenue toward Roosevelt Road. In less than 10 minutes we were turning right on West Roosevelt and then a few blocks down another right into the FBI building parking lot. Fortunately, Special Agents Wright and Marek were at their desks and waiting for us.

We made our way to the now familiar office. Agent Marek met us at the doorway, and we were shown in and took our usual seats. I related our experience with the alleged car bomber, Oren Clanton, and his blustery talk of some kind of major attack on our legal system, the binding fabric of our society. And, that we were wondering whether the FBI had any information that would give credence to Clanton's boasting.

Agent Wright responded. "There are some developments that do indicate a big uptick in truck and multi-level multi-vehicle carrier traffic all over the North Side. Other reports indicate increased volume of motor vehicles being offloaded from the car carriers and freight rail lines going to not only major ports like New Orleans which would not be unusual, but also to secondary ports like Gulfport Mississippi. We also have intelligence sources that do show a big push for recruitment and organizing on the Internet.

"Do you have any credible intelligence about specific threats or a timeline?" I asked.

Teresa Marek answered. "We are getting some useful intel from our person in the First Patriot organization, but he is still stuck at a lower level in the group. They are very cautious, and he hasn't been with them long enough to have access to the inner workings or highest ranking members. He has learned some interesting things, though. They are low on funds and desperate to see some big payoff from the car theft business that they have been engaging in with the Russians. And another thing he has discovered, the white supremacists and the Russians don't trust each other."

Elaina had another question. "Jack and I are used to being in tough situations. We have been threatened, shot at, assaulted and now an attempted car bombing. But, what we aren't accustomed to are threats against our families, our kids for Christ sake! I know that I speak for Jack, when I say that we are willing to do whatever it takes to bring these loco criminals down. And I do mean whatever it takes. Please keep us informed, as much as you possibly can."

"We will detectives." Teresa Marek stated intensely. "Whatever we can. Whatever it takes. We promise!"

Chapter 19

Wednesday morning began calmly enough, but for some reason I felt unsettled and anxious. Elaina and I were eager to finally interview Patti Vail and the lack of any new threats or noticeable activity from the First Patriot group or the Russians made me a little nervous. And, I don't get nervous. I could sense that Paige felt it too.

We had settled into a routine of us living together, leaving for work in the morning and then meeting up at her office at the end of the day and going back to my apartment. Tuesday, we stopped by her place first, so she could get her mail and a couple of wardrobe changes to last her for a few days. I was enjoying her company in a way that I hadn't felt for a long time. She was a much better cook than I was, and she helped me to change the dressing on my knife wound and rewrap it every evening. It still caused me some discomfort, but it was healing.

In the back of my mind, I worried that the arrangement wasn't realistic. Our jobs were both demanding and required us to work long hours including nights and weekends. And when she informed me that her team at the State's Attorney's Office had been assigned to prosecute Oren Clanton, my anxiety level skyrocketed. She was already receiving threats over the Billy Sims case, and now she could have become a target for the crazy supremacists. I couldn't help thinking what the hell is next.

It didn't take long for what came next. Shortly after Paige and I entered onto Lakeshore Drive, my phone buzzed and I heard the distinctive base voice of Lieut. Tyrone Whitehead. "Where the hell are you, detective?" he roared.

"I'm on Lakeshore Drive heading into the station." I answered.

"Well, stay on the Drive and put your emergency blue light on! You'll run into heavy action around Chicago Avenue. You better get off at North Avenue and get on the Inner Drive, or you will get stuck in the traffic. It's already been closed at Chicago Avenue. One of your father's lawyers just got shot at and run off the fucking road. I think it's Linda Prassas. You know her?"

"Yeah I know her Lieutenant. She works with my dad and is a friend. She was the lead defense attorney on the Billy Sims case. She has been getting threats, since she filed a notice of appeal on the case. Is she okay?"

"I don't know Jack. Get your ass down there and keep me informed. Rodriguez will meet you there."

So, I put my blue light on and gave Paige a quick call to tell her to get off Lakeshore Drive and head away from the lake to get to her office.

By the time I got on the Inner Lakeshore Drive, the traffic was already backing up going south, so I began weaving in and out of the oncoming lane, until I got about a block away from Chicago Avenue and the police perimeter. From there it was blocked off by a squad car and several officers, one of whom approached my driver side window, I flashed my badge and told him to move the patrol car to let me into the crime scene. He got into the car and pulled it forward to let me pass, and then backed it up into place. About 1/2 a block down the street was clogged with other patrol cars, an ambulance and a fire truck. I found an opening about 20 yards from the ambulance and parked my Camaro.

As I walked toward the scene, I saw my partner approaching from the other direction. She must have parked somewhere on Chicago Avenue, I thought. We arrived at the back of the ambulance at the same time and could see the EMTs loading a stretcher with a woman wearing a neck brace and sling holding her left arm in a tight position pinned to her chest.

I recognized Linda Prassas immediately and got a sickening feeling in my stomach. I couldn't help envisioning the snarling face of Oren Clanton. Here was another attack on a member of the legal profession. This time It was a defense attorney, but it didn't seem to matter. It could just as easily have been a prosecutor or a cop.

"Hold on guys. Give us a minute with your passenger." Elaina didn't need any explanations from me. The EMTs stood back and we jumped into the back of the bus to speak with the victim. Linda Prassas didn't need any introductions. I had known her for 15 years, and she had met Elaina a couple of times at my dad's house.

Prassas looked at me and winked, as she smiled. I remembered having always liked her and even having a crush on her as a teenager. She was attractive but mostly just really cool. "Are you okay to talk Linda?" I asked. "We just need to ask a few questions."

"Sure Jack. This is one time when talking to the police will be a pleasure." She said laughing somewhat uncomfortably. "You know the old saying. It really does hurt when I laugh." She chuckled again accompanied by another pained look. "Hi there, Detective Rodriguez. Nice to see you too."

"Likewise." Elaina responded. "What the hell happened?"

"I was taking my usual ride to work on the Drive in normal traffic. I love being by the lake in the morning. Even just seeing it from the road a little bit is a nice start to the day. There was nothing unusual, until out of nowhere this silver truck charged up and rammed into my back end sending me spinning, and then after I did a complete 360 in the middle of the highway, somehow I managed to avoid getting hit by the traffic coming behind me, until this maniac sped up and ran right into the driver side of my car causing it to flip over and crash into the concrete barrier. After that, I must have blacked out for a while. The next thing I knew I was being treated by the EMTs. Thank God for them!"

"I know how fast things happen Linda. But did you get the make and model of the truck?", I inquired. "Or recognize the driver?".

"You know I'm not much on cars or trucks. But I think it might have been a Ford, what model I have no idea. The driver was a white guy with light brown hair. That's about it I'm afraid. I hope that helps. Go get the bastard will you! This is one case that the Public Defender's Office won't touch. We'll be rooting for the prosecution." Linda Prassas laughed and winced again, as we jumped off the bus and the EMTs jumped on and closed the doors.

"It sounds like the guy that ran her off the road is the same asshole that we chased away from my dad's BBQ and who was at Cheryl Greenberg's service and gave me this slice in my side a few days ago. I would really like to get my hands on that chicken shit jagoff!

Elaina said something passionately in Spanish and then, "If he or any of those Bastardos come near my kids, I won't hesitate to finish it, Jack. Comprende?"

"Yeah partner, I comprende. Let's check in at the station and then head up to Wilmette and talk to the elusive Patti Vail."

A few minutes later we walked into our headquarters on N. Larrabee St. and then directly to Lieut. Whitehead's office. Whitehead was always a serious man, but he seemed particularly grim on this morning. He motioned for us to sit. We briefed him on the Linda Prassas situation and our plan to interview Cheryl Greenberg's close friend Patti Vail in hopes of learning more about our victim and to find out her laptop password. The Lieutenant was the only one who knew that we had her computer.

After that we had a meeting with Detectives Latner, Sanchez, Baker and Makris. There were no major developments concerning the murders of Judge Eggleston and witness Jay Farrell. They were still reviewing closed-circuit videos from various cameras and canvassing for more witnesses. There were no useful forensic discoveries and no luck finding the work truck used by Judge Eggleston's killer. The same was the case in our search for the silver Ford F150.

By 10 AM we were in our assigned gray Chevy Malibu for another trip up Lakeshore Drive on the way to Wilmette and the Michigan Shores Club. I took that time to call my dad who, of course, had been made aware of the attack on Attorney Linda Prassas. So, I let him know that we were able to see her before she was taken to the hospital and that she was seriously injured but was still her smart-ass self. He seemed somewhat relieved and said that he was on his way to Northwestern Memorial Hospital to see her. I was worried about his safety, and I knew that he was worried about mine. We both left it at that.

We verified with Margaret that Aquatics Director Patti Vail was indeed at work that morning before making the now familiar drive up to the North Shore. It was another sunny and mild September day, and we could see the Wilmette Beach on the right, as we turned left onto Michigan Avenue and parked across from the club entrance.

Margaret was her usual cheerful self, as she greeted us like old friends before picking up the phone at the reception counter and calling Ms. Vail. A minute later a tall athletic looking woman with shortcut blonde hair literally bounced around the corner and walked briskly toward us. She wasted no time introducing herself and directed us to follow her to a sitting area in the lobby that offered us some measure of privacy. Neither Elaina or I were surprised to learn that she was the head swimming coach of the Michigan Shores team that produced many of New Trier's top swimmers, and that both she and Cheryl Greenberg had swam there before also being teammates at New Trier.

We expressed our condolences about the loss of her close friend and our appreciation in advance for any help she could give us in finding the killer or killers and bringing them to justice. Hearing that was clearly evoking an emotional response, as her eyes welled up, and it took her a moment to regain her composure. "Thank you detectives. It's hard to express how deeply Cheryl's loss has affected me. Old friendships are so special and impossible to replace. And, we have been best friends since sixth grade. I have a hard time referring to her in the past tense.

Elaina reached out and placed her hand on Patti Vail's left arm and said something softly in Spanish followed by, "the people who did this to your amiga are terrible ruthless criminals. We think that they have killed others and are threatening to kill many more. They have threatened both of us and our families. We intend to stop them before that happens, and we think you may be able to help us."

"Anything." Patti Vail responded. "Whatever I can do to help you've got it!"

"We found Cheryl's laptop. It wasn't until days after her murder, and it seems that whoever killed her was looking for it too. They want it bad. They ransacked the Greenberg's house and cars and Cheryl's apartment and office looking for it. We think Cheryl's partner Matt Giordano was also murdered by the same people when they broke into their offices looking for it."

"Oh, you looked under the car seat", Patti said with a little laugh. "She has been doing that with her laptop since high school."

"At first it was just kid stuff. She never wanted her parents or sisters to get into it, so when she got a used car in her junior year at New Trier, she thought of using Velcro on the bottom of the driver side car seat and on the back of her laptop. Then after she became an attorney, she would still do that, whenever she had it in the car with her, just in case she wanted to leave it in there, when she was going out or in case she got mugged or something. Pretty prophetic, huh."

"Yes, it was prophetic, unfortunately, but it could be a big break for us." I added. "The problem we are having is that we can't get into it. We don't have the passcode. Do you have any insight as to what it might be?"

Patti Vail's eyes lit up." I can do much better than that. I know exactly what it is. It was our little secret, we both use the same one. It's SwimTrevians99"

"What's that again? What is a Trevian?" I asked.

"Okay. I know it's a little bit unusual. Trier is a city in Germany that was built during the Roman Empire and was a big deal for a while. People from Trier were called Trevians in Latin. We were freshman on the swim team in 1999, so we thought SwimTrevians99 was clever, I guess." And she laughed again. "I hope that helps."

"Oh mio Dios, yes!" Elaina proclaimed. "This could be just what we need. Thank you so much. But we must ask one more thing from you. There may be some other people calling or coming to you asking the same questions. They could even be other detectives. These may be extremely dangerous people. Please do not tell them anything about the computer. It's too late to deny that we have been here. Margaret knows, and others have seen us. Just say we were asking whether Cheryl had any boyfriends or enemies, things like that. Don't say anything more. And be careful."

We thanked Coach Vail again and waved at the ever-smiling Margaret on the way out. Our excitement was overflowing. I didn't even have to suggest a course of action. Elaina headed straight for the Covington Apartments, where the laptop waited for us in my apartment.

Chapter 20

We couldn't seem to get to my place fast enough. And while brimming with excitement, I couldn't shake a lingering anxiety. What will we do, if the password doesn't work? At the apartment, I pulled it down from my bedroom closet and placed it on the kitchen table, where for a few seconds we both stared at it without saying a word.

Finally, Elaina nodded at me, and I opened the laptop and typed in SwimTrevians99. Then voilà! The screen filled with a wallpaper photo of Glencoe Beach, numerous icons and a ribbon full of options. We moved closer together, so that we could both see the screen and began consulting on how to best determine which files and folders to open.

It took us about 1/2 an hour before we hit on the Victor Kirilenko files. Cheryl Greenberg had a habit of cryptically naming her files, and Kirilenko's was no exception. She had labeled them under "Darth." It seems that she viewed her client in the same way that we were seeing all of the participants in the radically charged carjacking scheme.

Attorney Greenberg's Kirilenko folder contained at least a dozen separate files containing court documents, discovery from the State's Attorney's Office, various filings from her law firm on behalf of Victor Kirilenko and a number of files that were not labeled. So, it was very time-consuming to wade through the stuff, until we got to some files that really got our attention. We hit on some containing written notes from Greenberg's meetings with her client and the prosecutors.

Unfortunately, attorney Greenberg's notetaking style was as cryptic as her file labeling. So, reading through dozens of pages from her interviews with Kirilenko was difficult and tedious. Elaina and I devised a process, where I would read one paragraph at a time out loud, and then we could try to determine what if anything was relevant and important enough for us to take our own notes on a legal pad that I kept around to occasionally use for phone call messages.

The first few pages were mostly general conversation about the multiple criminal charges, possible penalties and evidence that the State's Attorney's Office had against him. While we found his extensive criminal activities to be interesting, much of it dealt with Russian mob business such as extortion, kidnapping and the murder of other Russian gangsters. We agreed that this was one really bad dude, but so far we hadn't seen any involvement and our cases.

Then the subject of the conversations changed. For the first time, I saw the words First Patriots. It came up in relation to the subject of carjacking charges. Greenberg's notes were somewhat hard to decipher, but they indicated that Kirilenko admitted that the Russians he was affiliated with, were dealing with a group of Americans that he referred to as the patriot morons. It seems that the Russians really looked down on these guys but believed that the morons could make them a lot of money.

Then things got even more interesting again. The notes mentioned a plan to have the First Patriots steal hundreds of cars and trucks on the North Side and then filter them through a number of gas stations and auto shops in the Ukrainian Village and West Town areas, before bringing them to some large industrial and commercial facilities in Jefferson Park. They would then be brought down to ports on the Gulf of Mexico to be shipped out of the country and sold on the black market .

There were no more references to the actual car theft operation. But Kirilenko did make several more references to the First Patriots who he labeled as stupid but dangerous. He also revealed that they had members in both the Chicago Police Department and the State's Attorney's Office. That revelation really caused us both to sit back and say "Whoa!"

Here's where Cheryl Greenberg's secretive notetaking really got frustrating for us. The next few pages were full of short phrases and references to meetings that Victor Kirilenko had with mob associates and victims who were being extorted by him.

Then Cheryl's last page of notes got really opaque. There was just a string of phrases and scatterings of names, initials and just single letters which seem to be referring to people that her client had met or communicated with. The most notable and troubling of which were ones that indicated meetings with Chicago PD personnel and at least one prosecutor from the State's Attorney's Office followed by the letters TT.

There were several more references to Chicago PD without any hint at who the notes refered to. One of the phrases simply stated that there was a meeting scheduled on July 11 at 7 PM with Chicago PD and NO showed. Neither Elaina or I were sure whether there was a reference to a person, or if it was a no-show. But Greenberg's last phrase was clear. "Can't trust the Chicago PD or State's Attorney's Office. Contact FBI."

The next group of files were all marked as Kirilenko audio recordings. We opened the first one, and when we listened to it, the entire conversation was between a couple of men speaking what to me sounded like Russian or some other Eastern European language. We opened a few more of these files and heard the same type of conversations. Well, Elaina didn't know any more about was being said than I did. Luckily, we knew someone who did. It was time to follow Cheryl Greenberg's advice and contact the FBI.

It was just before 4 PM, and I didn't hesitate to put a call in to Agent Teresa Marek's cell phone. She picked up quickly and said she was glad that I called, and that there were some new developments that we needed to know about.

"That's quite a coincidence." I responded. "I think we have something important for you too. Are you and Agent Wright at your office?"

"No. We just wrapped up an interview and we are on our way back. We are about 20 minutes away."

I grabbed the laptop, and we went to the parking area in my building and Elaina took to the wheel. The traffic was moderately heavy on Lakeshore Drive as well as Roosevelt Road after we exited and drove west to the FBI Headquarters. It was closer to 25 minutes, and when we arrived, we learned that Agents Marek and Wright had preceded us.

We walked into their office without knocking and placed the laptop on Teresa Marek's desk right in front of her. She looked at me smiling. "Some pretty hot stuff, huh."

"It's dynamite. You guys are already aware that this Kirilenko dude is quite the bad ass. But Cheryl Greenberg's notes made it clear that the Russians are definitely fully involved in the carjacking scheme with the First Patriots, and that the group has people in the Chicago PD and the State's Attorney's Office. Greenberg didn't trust anybody and was ready to come to the FBI, before she and Kirilenko got taken out. But there are also at least a dozen files of conversations between Kirilenko and other Russians that he must have secretly recorded. I can't wait to hear what you get out of those."

"Well, you weren't joking, detective. We will get on those files right away. I may need to bring in another Russian-speaking agent to speed up the process."

"No problem Agent Marek." I said. "You're the doctor. No one at Chicago PD knows we have it except our Lieutenant. We don't know, who we can trust either. Have you guys come up with anything on any of the carjacking task force detectives?"

This time Special Agent Tony Wright answered. "Yeah, we dug pretty deep on all of them and really didn't find much other than a few youthful indiscretions such as a couple of drunk driving arrests and several youth offender assaults. But there was one thing we uncovered that got our attention. I think you mentioned that you have had some contact with a Detective Oscar Anderson?"

"You might say we know him and his partner." Elaina snapped." They're not the easiest people to like. What have you got?"

"They may not be the easiest to trust either." Said Agent Wright. "It seems that our Detective Oscar Anderson is really Detective Nikita Orlov. His parents emigrated to Chicago from St. Petersburg in 1990 when he was seven, and he legally changed his name when he turned 18 just before he enlisted in the U.S. Army and served four years before going into the Chicago PD in 2006. He made detective in 2014. There's not much after that other than a few complaints of excessive force that never went anywhere."

"Did you say Nikita Orlov?" I wanted to make sure that I heard it right.

"Yeah Jack. You heard it right." Teresa Marek confirmed." Is the name familiar to you? "

"No not the name. It's the initials. NO. There is a reference of a meeting between Kirilenko and the Chicago PD followed by a date in July and the letters NO. We aren't sure if that referred to someone, or whether it meant no one showed up. I guess we're still not sure, but I think the odds just shifted in the direction of Detectives Anderson and Solar."

"We will look further into that." Agent Marek noted." But we have some news of our own. Our agent inside the First Patriot organization has made some progress. He has managed to get close to a couple of members who have some standing in the upper echelons of the group, and he has been brought into some of the operational activities. These guys have started to open up to him and include him at some social gatherings, where the beer and whiskey and information has flowed."

"That is excellent!" Elaina exclaimed. That captured my feelings exactly. Things were starting to move, and I was ready to spring into action. "What has he been able to find out?"

"For one thing, these guys are much farther along in their grand plan than we thought. They have been stealing and jacking cars for over a year and began by selling small numbers of them around the city for resale or for parts to fund their group. As time went on, they started selling regularly to the Russian mob and that proved more lucrative for both sides. Eventually, they cooked up a plan for one huge deal that would get the radical group the resources they need and provide the Russians a big payday."

"Wow! How far along are they?" Elaina wanted to know.

Agent Marek continued. "Too far, I'm sorry to say. They were able to amass over a thousand late-model cars and trucks and stash them in large facilities mostly on the Nortwest Side of Chicago before moving them by rail and large car carriers down to Gulfport Mississippi to be shipped in containers on massive cargo vessels to Cuba and Venezuela."

"That's great to get this intel." I said.

"Well, yes and no." Agent Wright responded. "Yes, we now know what the plan is but no, because we got this Intel too late to stop the first part of it. The cargo ships have actually left the port and are in international waters. The Russians have been using cloaking technology on cargo ships to get them around sanctions put in place after the Ukraine invasion, and it seems that the Russian mob here has been able to use simpler versions of it to block the tracking of stolen vehicles. That's why they have seemed to disappear once they get to the Ukrainian Village area.

"Damn! What is the second part of their plan?"

Teresa Marek answered me. "We are still working on getting the details. Our inside man has to tread lightly. He has to let the information come to him. It is something ominous and on a large-scale. That's all we have right now. We'll keep you informed."

It was after 5 PM, when we left the FBI building and drove to our station. I called Paige and left a message that I was on my way after picking up my car. Even with everything that was on my mind, I was still excited about seeing her.

Elaina and I reported to Lieut. Whitehead who was fine with our decision to turn Cheryl Greenberg's laptop over to the FBI and told us to continue our cooperation and to watch our backs. We gave each other a high-five in the parking lot and then went on our separate ways.

When I got to the State's Attorney's Office I was waived in and went directly to Paige's new office that was down a long hallway next to her fellow teammates Tara Thistle and Jason Smith. Walking past one of the conference rooms I noticed that Paige was sitting at a table with attorney Terrance Goggins and another lawyer that I didn't recognize.

Paige looked up and saw me, but just gave a very slight move of her had in the direction of her office and so I kept going. Before I could enter into it, the conference room door opened and Terrence Goggins walked out followed by Paige and the other guy. They all looked tensed up. Even to a cop like me they looked unusually grim. Just then a young lawyerly looking woman walked up to them and said out loud: "The boss is looking for you TT. He seems really worked up about something."

"So what else is new?" Goggins responded, before following her down the hall.

Paige turned and headed right toward me. She broke out into a wide smile, when our eyes met, and for a brief pleasant moment all the BS faded away. Once inside her office she closed the door, and we entered into a warm exilerating embrace. Of course, it couldn't last long. There was a knock on the door, and in walked the leader of the team, Attorney Thistle.

"Sorry to interrupt you two." She said laughingly. "I am envious. But Paige and I need to discuss a couple of things, before you leave for the day."

"No problem." Paige replied with a smile. It was clear that the two were comfortable with each other which seemed to make for a good working relationship.

I offered to wait in the conference room, but Tara assured me that it was okay to stay. We were after all on the same side, she reminded me.

First, she asked Paige to tell her how the meeting with Terrance Goggins went. Paige explained that he just wanted to go over the game plan for responding to the Billy Sims appeal, once it was actually filed. He and Paige would need to assist whichever attorney from our appellate team got the case. But, since normally attorney Linda Prassas would have 90 days to file the formal appeal and because of her injuries that might get extended, there was nothing they could do about it now.

Then Tara informed Paige that she had scheduled a conference with Oren Clanton's attorney, Shelby Warren Gately, for the next morning at 9:30 AM. "That's fine." Paige noted. "Would you like me to attend?"

"No. I'd like you to handle it. I have to be in court on the Jenkins case. Anyway, I think you will get a kick out of old Shelby Warren Gately the third."

"Oh so you know this guy?" I wondered out loud.

"No, not really." Tara responded. "Just a couple of phone calls. He sounds a little different, if you know what I mean. You too can resume doing whatever it was, you were doing." She said, laughing again.

She walked out of the office closing the door behind her. And we gladly followed her directions.

Chapter 21

Thursday morning was quiet. Paige and I were settling into a comfortable albeit still very young relationship. Our morning routines were compatible, and the timing of our work day was in sync so far. But, in the back of my mind I knew that a detective's schedule was often long and irregular. That was troubling, but we just had to take each day as it came.

The previous evening at home had provided us with time to relax, but also to discuss the realities of what was going on in our lives. Paige was undaunted by the threats and was determined to forge ahead with her work as a prosecutor. She was happy to be on a new team and away from Terrance Goggins. She did have some interesting information concerning the senior prosecutor. As it turns out, his middle name is Timothy. Therefore, you have Terrance Timothy Goggins also known as TT.

I admired her strength, but I also was determined to do as much as possible to limit her exposure to potential danger. We agreed that for the time being she would not go back to her apartment by herself, and that we would leave for work and come home together whenever possible.

We left the apartment at 8 AM and lost each other as usual on Lakeshore Drive. I pulled into the station lot at 8:20 AM and could see Elaina had beaten me there. Also, as usual. By 8:30 AM our entire team was in the detectives' room, and we held a short meeting about our plans for the day. Zileen Baker and George Makris were focusing on possible suspects in the murder of Cheryl Greenberg, Matt Giordano and Jay Farrell other than people connected to Victor Kirilenko and the First Patriots. And Morgan Latner and Henrique Sanchez were concentrating on the killing of Judge John Eggleston. We could not rule out that there were other people with motives to go after him.

Elaina and I were going to continue to look at the First Patriots and their connection to the Russian mob. Our first stop that morning would be to the Near West Police Headquarters to talk to Detectives Beth Howard and Nick Salerno. We were aware that results from the FBI review of the Kirilenko Russian language conversations might not be available for a while. We were also going to do some digging in hopes of finding the silver Ford F150, driven by the knife wielding second man at the Greektown car bombing scene.

Lieut. Whitehead was out of the station that day, so after spending about 1/2 hour checking the most recent and pressing messages on other cases, we all headed out on the day. We were given a black Chevy Blazer, and about 20 minutes later Elaina had driven us into the parking lot of the Near West Police Station on South State Street.

We had called ahead, so when we checked in with the desk officer at the entrance of the bustling station, Officer Alessandro Testa directed us to room 312 on the third floor. When we got there, the door was open, and the large room was buzzing with detectives and officers coming in and out. There were phones ringing and the chaotic sounds of multiple conversations. Elaina and I couldn't help smiling at each other while looking for our detectives.

Finally, Beth Howard stood up from the far corner of the raucous room and waved for us to come over. We waded through the free-for-all and made it to the area, where she and Salerno had managed to squeeze into their desks. We waited for a couple of minutes, while they finished a heated conversation with a couple of uniformed officers who left looking like they were just ordered to round up the entire Gangster Disciples Gang and bring them in by 4 o'clock.

Detective Nick Salerno offered Elaina the one available chair and said dryly, "Nice to see you guys. Glad you picked a slow day to come in."

I chuckled and responded, "Yeah, the Near North was really crazy today. We needed to find a quiet place to do a little work."

"Okay then. Let's get to it. "Salerno said with a smile. We spent the next hour and 1/2 exchanging information and ideas about where to go next with the investigation into the car bombing and its connection to the larger threats posed by radical groups such as the First Patriots.

Agents from the Bureau of Alcohol, Tobacco and Firearms and Explosives had stopped by to see them after examining the blown up car and debris. They wouldn't be finished with their investigation for weeks, but they believed that the device was similar to others used in recent years in church and synagogue bombings. The explosives were of the same type as quantities stolen from Fort Campbell which straddles the borders of Kentucky and Tennessee.

Salerno and Howard had also interviewed numerous people that they already were aware of having ties to various white supremacist organizations in Chicago and the Midwest. Most were uncooperative as expected, but they found a couple who were willing to speak off the record.

One guy reported that he was a former member of the First Patriots but had left the group a couple of months ago, when they began talking about and actually planning some large-scale violence. He was okay with stealing cars and their views on white supremacy, but he felt that since the arrival of some new more radical guys from Mississippi he decided to bail out.

I asked whether this guy had mentioned any names of the new Mississippi players and was told that the guy couldn't remember the names of most of them, but two had stood out to him. They were our boy, Oren Clanton, and another scary character named Lester Shelton. He was described as a tall wiry man about 35 years old with sandy or light brown colored hair and a very pale complexion. There was no doubt in my mind who Lester Shelton was. He was a very dangerous bastard with a pronounced limp.

We wrapped up our meeting with the Near West detectives, and when we left, the atmosphere in the room hadn't changed much. The noise level required Nick Salerno to yell after us as we left. "By the way Jack, we were at Oren Clanton's arraignment yesterday. The nut job wouldn't shut up. He kept on spewing all kinds of threats toward the judge, the police and even his own lawyer. But he seemed especially focused on you and everyone close to you. You know, your partner, your family and he specifically mentioned your colored girlfriend. Just thought you should know. Watch your back buddy."

I waved and turned to Elaina. "He's right of course. We do need to watch our backs. But, if I get a chance at Lester Shelton first, I can't guarantee that he'll be legally dead. He'll just be dead." My partner replied something to me in Spanish. I wasn't sure about all the words, but I was sure of the look in her eyes.

We weren't far from the Ukrainian Village neighborhood, so Elaina drove a few blocks west to Western Avenue and turned right. 15 minutes later we were in the area, where so many stolen vehicles had been tracked and then mysteriously seemed to disappear. Our plan was to stop at every gas station and garage that could accommodate even one car or truck and to try to speak to whoever we could find, and ask to look around the place.

We stopped by five places and found nothing unusual or suspicious. No one refused to speak with us, even though a couple of times the gas stations were run by either Ukrainians or Russians that hadn't exactly mastered the English language yet. Still, they allowed us to look around and even look at their service records for the past couple of months. Nothing stood out.

Nothing, that is, until we stopped by an independent gas station, the R&M near the corner of Augusta Boulevard and Damon Avenue. Right away the large size of the service garage with three extra wide bay doors seemed out of place. Next to the single gas pump and tiny office there was no Stop & Shop to the place, and as far as we could see, there were no cars being serviced inside the garage. There was one employee inside, and he was of as little help as possible.

When we parked in front of the office, we could see a man sitting at a desk inside, and he never even looked up from his phone. Sitting there for about 10 minutes, we didn't see any sign of action inside or out. There was plenty of street traffic, but none of it turned into the R&M Station.

Finally, we got out of the Blazer and went inside the office. Still there was no reaction from the lump of a guy sitting behind the desk. I wrapped my knuckles on the counter and the guys head jerked up, and he seemed startled to see somebody at the station. He recovered enough to ask us what we wanted.

We introduced ourselves and asked him what was going on. He said that his name was Demetri, and that he was the only one there and that the station was closing down. The owners had recently decided to sell the property and move back to Russia.

"That seems kind of sudden." I observed. "Are the owners here now? And who are they by the way?"

"No. Mr. Radovich and Mr. Makarov are not here. They just have me watching place until it sold."

"Do you expect to see them today?" Elaina inquired.

"No not today." Demetri responded. "I never expect to see owners. They tell me look after place until it sell. So that is what I do."

"When did they shut the station down?" I asked.

"Shut it all down. That's all I know. No more gas. No more cars. Nothing. It is all gone in one day. Maybe they homesick. They don't tell me nothing. Just stay here. Look after place."

We both felt like this had to be checked out further right away. The databases on our computers at the station were calling us home. So, the rest of the potential car theft shelters would have to wait. About 15 minutes later we were sitting at our desks checking out the R&M gas station and Mr Radovitch and Mr. Makarov.

It didn't take long for some very interesting results to pop up. It seems that good old Sergei Radovich and Igor Makarov were frequent flyers in the criminal justice system. They both had long rap sheets in New York including violent assaults and possession of stolen property, before moving to Chicago a couple of years earlier.

They were known to have connections to the Russian mob in Brighton Beach, Brooklyn. They were in the Country legally and had kept a low profile since coming to Chicago.

Elaina concentrated on researching the R&M gas station, and the most interesting thing was what she didn't find. The business was held by a shell corporation that was owned by another shell corporation that was held in a blind trust. It had a license to operate as a business in Illinois and Chicago, but there were no overt signs of any business activity.

My next move was to call Special Agent Teresa Marek to see if the FBI had anything on these guys. Teresa picked up my call and said that they were out and involved in something that would keep her and Agent Wright busy well into the evening. She said that the Kirilenko recordings were being translated by other Russian-speaking agents. She thought that she should have the transcripts by early in the morning and asked us to come by the office at 10 AM.

As soon as I hung up with Agent Marek, my phone buzzed, and I saw that it was Paige. The tone of her voice was alarming. She had just returned to her office from 26th and California, where she and Tara Thistle were conducting a pretrial hearing in an armed robbery case. But that wasn't what had her upset. It was the fact that two men carrying bags of sandwiches and soft drinks tried to get through security before being stopped and engaging in a violent brawl with security guards.

My mind started racing. I was used to being under pressure and threats in my job and other situations, while growing up in Chicago, but I wasn't used to being so worried about the people closest to me. "Paige, are you all right? How far did they get into the building?"

"They got to the elevators before the security officers stopped them and they then attacked the guards with knives. Two guards were stabbed and a third was knocked down and kicked. The two bolted for the exit, but one was shot in the head on the way out and died at the scene. The other guy ran into a waiting car and got away. Witnesses said he got into a blue Ford F150 truck and that he was noticeably limping."

"Did they lock down the building?" I asked.

"Well, they did for about an hour and 1/2 and security was increased, but people had to keep working. Tara and I had to go to court or a really dangerous guy would have walked. You know how it goes, Jack"

"Yeah. I know. That's what bothers me. It's almost 5 PM. Let me finish up here, and I'll be by to get you. Stay there."

"I'll be here. Don't worry baby. We don't even know where these guys were going, or who they were after."

"Yeah but I do, babe. I'll be right there."

When I exited the elevator on the 12th floor, the hallway was busy as usual and I saw the carjacking task force detectives leaving Paige's office with Attorney Thistle right behind them. I guess I wasn't invited to this meeting, I thought. Not that I wanted to be except to observe Detectives Anderson and Solar. My training taught me not to jump to conclusions, but something about these guys was off. Way off. And we were looking for an N.O. Person. It was not a stretch to think that it could be Nikita Orlov, a.k.a. Oscar Anderson.

I had to literally brush past them in the crowded hallway, and the other detectives, Weber, Del Bacaro, O'Brien and Nijinsky nodded, while Anderson and Solar scowled. No problem. It was expected at that point. Tara Thistle smiled and greeted me with an invitation to join Paige in the office.

On the way there I also had the pleasure of passing Attorney Terrance Timothy Goggins who favored me with another dirty look. I smiled. No love lost there either. He and his buddies could go to hell for all I cared.

Inside the team's office, Paige and Jason Smith were at their desks working at their computers. Paige stood up and came around to greet me with a restrained handshake and an unrestrained smile. Just the feeling of her warm handshake sent a hot charge throughout my body. I was still in awe of the effect she had on me.

She needed some time to finish whatever she was doing on her computer, so I took a nearby chair and looked at my phone's most recent emails and texts until Attorney Thistle came back into the office and wanted to talk.

"Sorry you came a little late to sit in on that meeting Jack. Your buddies put on quite a show. This time they almost came to blows with Weber and Del Bacaro. That Anderson is really some piece of work. And his partner is no prize either. We usually have a great working relationship with all the detectives. It's making me uncomfortable every time we get a carjacking case now. How are things with you Jack?"

"Well, we have our own problems with the carjacking surge. We are focusing more on the bigger picture including our homicide cases that are connected. Right now, I'm more concerned with the safety of my family and Paige more than anything else."

"We take the threat seriously here too, detective. But the note she had left on her desk is very disturbing. I hate to think it could have come from someone in the State's Attorney's Office, but I do know there is some friction between Paige and Terrance Goggin's team. I had a talk with Goggins, and things seem to have calmed down. But, let me know if you need anything. I live nearby if Paige needs me."

"Thanks Tara. We will keep that in mind." Paige looked up when I said that and smiled, shutting down her computer, taking me by the arm and walking me out of the office.

Chapter 22

Friday morning arrived early for both of us after a restless sleep, during which we both tossed and rolled around much of the night. We did our best to have a normal night, having a nice dinner once again prepared by Paige and relaxing to some mellow music to keep our minds off the serious nature of the threats. But, neither of us succeeded.

Around 6 AM Paige suggested that we go for a run. I didn't even know that running was part of her repertoire. The wound in my side was healing well, but the doctor still advised against any strenuous exercise such as heavy lifting or basketball. Walking and jogging were okay, so we donned some shorts, T-shirts, and running shoes and headed out into the unusually warm mid-September morning.

Unlike during most of my runs around the neighborhood, I put my Beretta 9 mm in my pocket, and it felt awkward, but it reminded me that even while enjoying the simplest of life's pleasures, we needed to be prepared for anything. It sucked. But the alternative could be far worse.

I could see right away that she was a fluid and experienced runner. She was like a thoroughbred being held back by a pack mule. It was hard to limit myself to a moderate jog. Paige eventually settled into a slower rhythm, so we jogged through the park and down to Montreux Beach, where we took our time walking along the shore and enjoying the light breeze which was pushing the rippled surface water up onto the shoreline. It was a welcome serenity that we enjoyed for around 20 minutes before jogging back to the Covington Apartments.

Back home we showered together, as had become our habit, and then made love in the bedroom. It was difficult not to get carried away by how perfect everything seemed at that moment. Hardly a word was said. The way we looked at each other told us that we were feeling the same thing. The natural high lasted all the way, up until we got into our cars and drove out of the building and into the wonderfully terrible reality that is the great city of Chicago.

I kept her in front of me on the Lakeshore Drive until inevitably we became separated, and then she was gone and out of sight. Driving into the parking lot at the station I was briefly overcome by a powerful sense of melancholy and anxiety. I'm not sure exactly how long I sat there, but a rapid tapping on my driver side window snapped me out of it. It was my partner, Elaina.

"Are you all right amigo?" she asked with a genuine tone of concern.

"Yeah partner. I'm okay. Just daydreaming for a minute. You know. So much going on."

"Comprende. But we need to get with it to get on top of these bastards. Yes?"

"Si!!" I responded with enthusiasm. "Let's go get 'em!"

We walked into the detectives' room and quickly jumped onto our computers to try to clear up as many loose ends as possible, before going to our meeting at FBI Headquarters. The first thing I did was to modify the BOLO on the silver Ford F150 truck, to include the possibility that it may now have been painted dark blue. My biggest personal and professional priority was to find the people that had been threatening me, my partner and my family.

By 9 AM all of the other team members had reported in, and we decided to have a quick meeting before Elaina and I left to see Agents Wright and Marek. Detectives Baker and Makris were chasing down some promising leads on possible people with grudges against attorneys Giordano and Greenberg, while Detectives Latner and Sanchez were doing the same concerning Judge Eggleston.

Elaina and I were very anxious to get together with our FBI partners and to find out what they had learned from the Victor Kirilenko recordings. We checked out the same Chevy Blazer we had the day before, and by 9:35 AM we were pulling into the FBI parking lot.

Up at their office Teresa Marek and Tony Wright were waiting for us, and I liked the look on their faces. "Sit right down guys." Agent Marek said. "We have a lot to go over, so we might as well dive right in."

We started with the recordings and the agents had broken them down into 15 separate files reflecting 15 conversations that Kirilenko had with other Russian mobsters over a period of almost a year.

The first 10 conversations were mostly significant because of details revealed about criminal enterprises that dealt with extortion, wholesale drug operations involving smuggling heroin into the US from Russian provinces and some illegal gambling operations. These were of great interest to the FBI and would be vigorously pursued, but they were only indirectly connected to our cases.

However, the last five conversations were right on point and chilling. The first one exposed how the partnership between these two seemingly diametrically opposed groups got started. The Russians were only minimally involved in car thefts around Chicago. They had a few chop shops such as the R&M gas station in Ukrainian Village, and then they were introduced to this group of radical white supremacists by someone in the Chicago PD that they referred to as N.O.

The supremacists wanted to start up a large-scale carjacking and theft operation to fund their group. They wanted to focus on the North Side, but didn't want to butt heads with the Russians or the Latin Kings. They felt like they could work with the Russian mob, but their racist views prevented them from working with any of the Latino gangs in the city. They would just stay out of Humboldt Park and a few other areas and count on the backing of the Russians everywhere else.

Other conversations dealt with setting up the operation, and specifically how it worked. The Russians were connected to criminal gangs inside Russia and had access to some of the technology that shipping operations were using to cloak their GPS locations, when engaging in large-scale shipping of products to and from Russia and certain allied countries to avoid the sanctions that were implemented after the invasion of Ukraine.

The Russians provided the garages and cloaking technology in the Ukrainian Village and surrounding neighborhoods. The First Patriots provided a steady stream of stolen cars and trucks. The vehicles were passed through to a couple of large buildings in Jefferson Park, one of which was a former bus garage for a transportation company that had gone out of business.

The cars and trucks were transported by train and large vehicle carriers provided by the Russians. They ended up in Gulfport Mississippi at the shipyards that were controlled by the Dixie Mafia who had a working relationship with the First Patriots.

Then, the last two conversations exposed the final plans which were both surprising and alarming. The idea was to ship vehicles down to Gulfport in a trickle at first and stockpiling them down there, while amassing a huge number of cars and trucks in Jefferson Park, until they were ready to perform a mass delivery down to the port for shipment into two large container vessels for delivery .

One of the ships would go to Venezuela and the other to Cuba. Unfortunately, that part of the plan had already taken place. But the second phase had yet to be completed and was the most troubling.

The Russians were strictly in it for the money. So, the shipment of vehicles going to Venezuela would produce cash that would entirely go to the Russian mob. The First Patriots, however, were in it for very different reasons. They only wanted enough money to promote their racist ideas, but what they did want were the resources needed to achieve a chaotic takedown of the existing social order. They wanted an anarchy that would cause a violent racial confrontation that would result in a new world order dominated by white supremacists.

Their plan was to begin by attacking the legal system and causing panic and confusion. They viewed all the people involved in law enforcement or the legal profession as the same. They all needed to be attacked, because they were the defenders of the current order.

The shipment of cars and trucks delivered to Cuba would produce military grade weapons and explosives that would be sent back to Gulfport on the same ship. The Russians were to provide the trucks and upon delivery back in Chicago, the money from Venezuela was going to be released to the Russians. It was clear that the Russians and the First Patriots didn't trust each other. The final details of the delivery of weapons and payment to the Russians was left open and would be determined later.

"These recordings have added a great deal of information that will be useful in ongoing investigations that we have concerning Russian organized crime activities. But our immediate focus is on what brought you two here today." Agent Wright commented. "The second part of the plan that was alluded to in the Kirilenko conversations is something that requires immediate action."

"Do we have any more specific Intel on the second part of their plan?" I asked.

Teresa Marek answered. "Thanks to our agent inside the supremacist group we now know that the ship containing weapons and explosives from Cuba has arrived at Gulfport Mississippi and will be unloaded sometime today. We do not think that we have enough time to get a search warrant in Mississippi, but we are working on getting one from the Northern District Federal Court here, once the trucks arrive at their destination in Chicago. Our guy inside hasn't been able to find out the exact location of the drop off site, other than it is on the Northwest Side somewhere."

"Is there any possibility that he can get the exact location before the shipment gets here?", Elaina inquired.

"Yes. There may be." Agent Marek continued. "Our agent has worked his way into the confidence of some group members who have substantial standing, but he unfortunately does not. However, he has learned that a very high-level meeting has been set up at a little out-of-the-way tavern in Ukrainian Village for tomorrow afternoon. These guys really don't trust each other, so they haggled over a neutral place to meet until they agreed on a little neighborhood place called Stella's. Do either of you know it?"

I practically jumped out of my chair. "You bet. I know the place. It's perfect. I used to go there during college, and I stopped in there a couple of weeks ago. I've got an idea. There's no way I can go back in there or any male agents. But if we put in a couple of good looking women dressed casually but attractively, we could get close enough to the Russians and First Patriots to overhear them or plant a listening device. What do you think?"

Agents Marek and Wright looked at each other quizzically. "Well, we don't have a lot of time or much choice. It could work if only we had a couple of nicelooking women to play the part." Tony Wright retorted with a laugh which we all shared.

This time it was Elaina Rodriguez's and Teresa Marek's turn to look knowingly at each other. "We can do this!", Elaina exclaimed. "No problem!" Teresa added.

The plan was set into motion. The FBI would handle the technical aspects including some creative listening devices and an undercover van, where Agent Wright and I would be stationed while Detective Rodriguez and Agent Marek spent a Saturday afternoon hanging out at Stella's Bar and Grill.

On the drive back to the station I was tempted to tell Elena to swing by Stella's to give Rita, the bar manager and primary bartender, a heads up about our plan, but I quickly dismissed that thought. For one thing, the Russians or First Patriots could already be keeping an eye on the place, and for another thing I didn't want Rita to know anything about our plan. She was a sweetheart but also a blabbermouth. There would be no way she could act naturally, if she knew what was going on.

So, we went directly back to the detectives' room while discussing what we had just learned and our plans for the next day. The warm weather was expected to hold on through Saturday before giving way to a cold front bringing possible storms. Elaina suggested that she and Agent Marek wear simple casual attire that would fit the working-class neighborhood but also accent their natural physical attributes. She thought that jeans and halter tops would do the trick.

I was impressed by how eagerly both women had embraced the idea of going undercover. But I was also apprehensive. One of the revelations from the FBI agent inside the supremacist group was still bothering me. It was that the tall thin guy that I had tussled with outside the Athena restaurant in Greektown, Lester Shelton. He had become obsessed with getting even with me. He had vowed to get me and everyone close to me. That, of course, included Elaina. I was worried about her going into a situation, where someone might recognize her.

Elaina was confident that with her long brown hair tied up and covered by a cowgirl hat and enticing makeup applied to her eyes and lips she wouldn't have men thinking about law enforcement. I could envision that working, as well as Teresa Marek also being attractive enough to be disarming to most men. As it turned out, they both liked to play pool, so they were going to fit in just fine at the down-to-earth neighborhood tavern.

Our conversation was interrupted, when my phone buzzed, and I heard my dad's voice on the other end. "Hey Jack I'm glad I caught you. Your brother Barry wants to have a little impromptu family gathering tonight at Smoke Daddy's in Wicker Park. Just a small group with myself, you and Molly. Can you make it?"

"I would like to dad. But, I will be with Paige Owira. You probably know her from the State's Attorney's Office. She has been staying with me. We've gotten close. She has been receiving threats too, so I'm trying to keep her safe whenever we're not at work."

"That's great Jack. Bring her along. I have seen her around 26th and California but have never talked to her. I would love to meet her. Can you make it by 6:30?"

"Yeah. We should be able to be there by 6:30. See you then. Watch your back, dad."

"You too, Jackie."

Chapter 23

Once we returned to the station on N. Larrabee St., our first stop was at Lieut. Whitehead's office. His initial reaction to our plan for Stella's Bar the next day was extremely negative to say the least. He not only felt that the operation was being put together too hastily, but that it was inherently too dangerous. We had no doubt about how violent the Russian mobsters and First Patriots were. And the best Elaina and Agent Marek could do to protect themselves was to have handguns in their bags. Agent Wright and I would have to park around the corner nearly a block away to avoid suspicion.

"Lieutenant, I understand your apprehension about sending Elaina into such a tricky situation, but this may be the only way to find out the exact location for the delivery of an arsenal of weapons that the FBI believes the supremacists group intends to use in some kind of large-scale attack on Chicago government buildings. That could include police stations. We wouldn't be doing this, if the threat wasn't so severe and so immediate. "

I could see from the look on Whitehead's face that he was starting to have a change of heart. "Okay, Detective Fallon. I don't want some kind of radical racist bloodbath on my hands. I will go along with this, but I want the rest of your team nearby in two separate unmarked cars. I can coordinate with District 12 to keep the patrol cars away from there tomorrow. I want to see the whole team tomorrow morning in my office at 10 AM. If it was anybody else, I'm not sure I would be okay this whole thing, but I have trusted you before. Just make it work and take care of yourselves."

We stood up and assured the Lieutenant that the plan was sound, and that we could handle it. He uncharacteristically stood up and shook our hands. The mood was serious, almost somber. This was a very risky, but absolutely necessary course of action.

Inside the detectives' room we huddled with our team members and laid out the plan of attack for Saturday. Everybody grasped the importance of what we were dealing with, and everyone was eager to do their part. There were no other detectives in the room at that time, and we all agreed to keep this operation totally to ourselves. We couldn't take a chance of word getting out to the carjacking task force or anyone else for that matter.

Saturday morning we would meet back at the station at 9:30 AM before our conference with Lieut. Whitehead at 10 AM. Later on, as we were all preparing to wrap up for the day, Morgan Latner suggested that we go over to Timothy O'Toole's for some beers, wings and the Cubs game. His girlfriend Tina was going out with her sisters in Evanston, and he was on his own. I didn't hesitate to invite him to join us at Smoke Daddy's on W. Division St. He readily agreed and said he would see us there at 6:30 PM.

Elaina and I exchanged a few parting thoughts, before going our own separate ways. She had plans in Pilsen for dinner at home with her husband Paco and her two little girls Rosie and Lucy. And I was on my way to collect Paige before going to the dinner in Wicker Park. The threats that we were all under and the looming violence aimed at our city and society magnified feelings we had for family and friends. The intensity of the moment made things crystal clear.

I had become such a familiar face at the County Offices Building that I was just waived in and onto the elevators up to the State's Attorney's Office. It was obvious that at 5:30 PM the lawyers were hustling around trying to tie up loose ends, before leaving for the weekend or at least until the next morning. Paige and her team partners, Tara Thistle and Jason Smith, were still at their desks when I walked in.

"Hi there detective." Tara said. "Paige let's wrap up for today. It looks like Jack is anxious to take you off somewhere. Besides, we are coming in tomorrow, so we can continue this then."

"Oh, you guys are working tomorrow? That's good, since I will be working too. Will you be working late? I'm not sure exactly when

I will be finished. I don't like the idea of Paige going back to my place herself."

"Don't worry Jack. If need be, I can take her home. It's not far out of my way and I don't mind at all."

"That's great Tara. I really appreciate it. I may be able to get here by 5 PM, but you know how police work goes."

"Yes I do, detective. Anything hot going on tomorrow?"

"No, just the usual stuff. I guess that's hot enough." I responded with a laugh.

Paige was unusually quiet and seemed to be preoccupied, almost as if she was dreading something. I couldn't blame her. I just hoped that a nice night out with the people closest to me would pick her up.

She gathered her things and we walked to the parking garage where her car was parked. We both got in and Paige drove me to my Camaro which was on the street about a block away. From there I followed her all the way back to my apartment building for a quick change of clothes, before heading out to Smoke Daddy's.

I threw on a Navy polo and khaki slacks, while Paige donned a scarlet short-sleeved blouse and tan linen pants. She looked amazingly beautiful even under such heavy stress. Just watching her climb into the passenger seat of my car made me feel lucky to have found her and to have her be a part of my life. I never wanted to lose her. I was ready to do anything to protect her.

We managed to arrive at the restaurant only about five minutes late. Everyone was there except sister Molly who was habitually tardy and was still on her way from Evanston. I made the introductions and was pleased to see, how warmly everyone received Paige. I purposely steered her next to my buddy Morgan and the two struck up a conversation right away. Morgan was not only my best friend and fellow detective, but he was also a product of a biracial marriage. Both he and Paige had an African American parent. Morgan's father was African American growing up in

Mississippi, and his mother was an Irish German American woman from Rogers Park and then Evanston.

Molly soon arrived, and she jumped right in and also formed a quick connection with Paige. My dad and brother Barry followed suit, and before long we were all enjoying beers and cocktails and telling stories like old friends. The BBQ was fantastic. The ribs and brisket lived up to the Smoke Daddy name, and two hours later everyone's appetite and thirst was well satisfied.

Barry, Molly and my dad wanted to keep the evening going at the Violet Hour Cocktail Bar on N. Damon Ave., but Paige and I were anxious to get back to my place and enjoy some alone time. Morgan had plans to catch up with his girlfriend Tina and her sisters at a bar in Evanston, so we all said our goodbyes with warm hugs and promises to do this again soon.

When we exited Smoke Daddy's, Morgan turned to walk west on Division Street while we turned left to walk east and around the corner to the Camaro parked on Wood Street. During our short walk Paige gushed about how comfortable she felt with my family and buddy Morgan Latner. I assured her that the feelings were mutual, bringing a wide smile to her face.

Once inside the car we kissed hotly, and she touched me causing a full rock-hard arousal. Only the presence of people on the street prevented us from going further right there. We later laughed, and I had to feign pleading with her to let me drive.

We pulled out onto Wood Street and then turned left on Division Street toward Lakeshore Drive. At that time on a Friday night the traffic was fairly heavy, but nothing unusual, until just past Ashland Avenue I noticed something startling.

A silver Ford F150 turned sharply in front of us from the outside lane and then slowed down. I strained to try to see the driver, but the tinted windows made it impossible. I could only imagine who it could be.

Then suddenly Wham! We were rear-ended by a blue truck. I was aware of the heavy traffic to my left so my reaction was to adjust to the right which caused the Camaro to sideswipe two parked cars. Sparks were flying, and I could feel that there was a problem with the front passenger side tire and wheel well.

Paige was terrified and began crying and holding onto my right side making it nearly impossible to steer the car. As it turned out that would soon be the least of my worries. The blue truck pulled around me and rammed us causing the Camaro to crash into more parked cars. This time the front right tire blew and our car spun around putting the rear end into the left lane. A passing Chrysler 300 slammed into us causing our car to spin 90°. We were now facing completely in the wrong direction.

The blue truck stopped directly behind us, and I could see the silver Ford F150 stopped just ahead of it. A man jumped out of the blue truck, and it looked like he had a gun in his hand. A second later when a bullet smashed through the rear window that was confirmed. I drew my Beretta and pushed Paige's head down. I had to fire across her body through the passenger side window at the figure approaching from behind us.

She screamed, and glass shattered everywhere. The figure outside the car went down but I wasn't sure what was going on with him. Next, another shot rang out, and a bullet went through the car into the screen. I yelled at Paige to stay down and tried to open my door but it was jammed. The next few seconds seemed like hours. We were sitting ducks. Then I saw a dark Buick sedan speed toward us and slam on the brakes. It was a sight for sore eyes. Morgan Latner jumped out with gun in hand and yelled at the top of his lungs,"Back off you scumbag, or I'll blow your fucking head off! Drop the fucking gun and knife right now!"

Then there was a silence, until Morgan appeared on the passenger side and leaned in. "Are you two okay? Is anyone hit?"

We heard the sound of a truck's tires peeling away. No buddy, I think we are all right." Paige sat upright shaking and crying. I took her into my arms and asked Morgan to call it in and ask for EMTs and a BOLO on the silver Ford F150.

"What's the story with the guy on the ground?" I asked.

I could see that Latner was kneeling down, probably to check on the condition of the assailant. When he stood up he just shook his head. "He's gone." Was all he said.

With Morgan's help we managed to get my driver side door open and Paige followed me out of the Camaro, having to step over a deceased middle-aged white guy of average height and weight. He had short brown hair, but there was nothing remarkable about him other than the hole in his chest.

"Did you get a good look at the other guy?" I inquired of Morgan.

"Yeah, I saw him clearly. He was a tall slender guy with sandy hair holding a long open switchblade with a white handle in one hand and a pistol in the other. He was coming hard for you two, but it was a little odd. He had a distinct limp. Does any of that sound familiar to you? "

"Oh yeah. That jagoff is Lester Shelton, one of the First Patriots assholes. He used that blade to slice me in Greektown last week.

"Damn!" Morgan responded. "If I had known that, I wouldn't have let him off the hook. I would've just blasted his ass."

I had to laugh a little which reminded me that the knife wound in my side was still bothering me. "Wouldn't have bothered me, buddy. If anybody deserves to be shot, that bastard does."

Within a couple of minutes Division Street was swarming with police cars and emergency vehicles. We all were interviewed separately by the responding detectives that both Morgan and I were familiar with as Dennis Cook and Mike Keenan from District 12. I noticed a few onlookers also being interviewed and was hoping that some of them had witnessed the whole thing.

They took my gun of course, but since I wasn't on duty the whole process would be a little less complicated. I wouldn't be immediately placed on administrative leave. It would be more of a standard criminal investigation. Detectives Cook and Keenan did their job and released us, pending further investigation. But, off the record, they both expressed that it seemed like a clear case of self-defense. I couldn't have agreed more.

Morgan gave us a ride back to my place, after we watched the Camaro being toted to a local body shop. I knew that it would be quite a while, before I drove my car again if they could even salvage it at all.

We both sincerely thanked Morgan for coming to the rescue. He said that he just had a feeling that he should follow us home for some reason. It wasn't really out of his way, and he trusted his gut. Thank God for that.

Paige and I were exhausted and ready for bed, as soon as we walked through the door. Neither of us slept much. She wrapped herself around me and wouldn't let me go. I didn't want her to. There wasn't any sex that night, but there was plenty of love.

Chapter 24

We began Saturday morning in slow motion. Both of us were still tired after short stretches of sleep and long periods of nervous meditation. We decided to skip our run and just enjoy a leisurely preparation for the day ahead.

Neither of us had much appetite, so we settled for some Catherine Clark's wheat toast and orange juice. We showered together as had become our habit. We lingered in the warmth of our long embrace and the water pouring down on us.

We were down to one car now, so Paige suggested that I drop her off at the County Building and take her car to the station. I agreed, partly because I thought I would be able to pick her up by 6 PM at the latest, but also because Attorney Tara Thistle had offered to take her home if need be.

The weather outside was warm and sunny which belied a forecast calling for a dramatic shift to much cooler temperatures and possible thunderstorms with heavy rain beginning overnight. But, for the time being, we were enjoying a summerlike cruise down Lakeshore Drive looking out at Lake Michigan and the lakefront parks filling up with weekend runners, walkers and bicyclists. It was hard not to enjoy the view which even brought a little smile to Paige's face.

Our enjoyment was short-lived, however, as we exited the Drive onto Michigan Avenue and made our way through the city traffic to the Cook County Building. It was a casual day at the State's Attorney's Office, so Paige was dressed comfortably in a short-sleeved white blouse and blue jeans. I was also dressed informally, since I would be out in the field with Agent Tony Wright on the street near Stella's in an undercover van, monitoring what was going on inside the bar.

Once at the County Building, we exchanged a brief hug and promises to see each other after work. I knew that staying in touch with her during the day would be difficult and unpredictable. I felt a little uneasy watching her walk away from the car and into the large office building. I just chalked it up to the whole damn situation which had been weighing heavily on us. Anyway, there was no time for being apprehensive. I had an important day ahead of me and a serious job to do.

When I got to the detectives' room at 9:15, Elaina was already at her desk as usual and Detective Henrique Sanchez was standing near the coffee maker talking to Detective Zileen Baker. We were waiting on Detectives Morgan Latner and George Makris to begin our meeting before our scheduled conference with Lieut. Whitehead.

After everyone arrived, we finalized the plan for the day. I would meet up with Special Agent Tony Wright in Ukrainian Village on a side street near Stella's. He would provide some kind of work van that has been converted into a mobile sound studio.

In the meantime, Elaina would go to the FBI Building to meet with Special Agent Teresa Marek. They were going to change into casual and somewhat revealing clothing that was appropriate for a warm September Saturday. The FBI informant reported that the meeting between the First Patriots and Russians was scheduled for 3 PM at Stella's.

Detectives Baker and Makris would station themselves in their unmarked car on a side street north of Stella's two or three blocks away, and Detectives Latner and Sanchez would do the same a few blocks south of the tavern.

Elaina and Teresa were planning on getting to Stella's around 2 PM and settling in at the bar. The idea was that by the time the targets got to the place they would be playing pool with beers in front of their seats, and they would know the bartender and some of the regulars by name.

At around 10 AM we went to our meeting with Lieut. Tyrone Whitehead to go over the details of the operation and to convince him that we were confident that we had it all covered before he gave his final approval.

It took me and the team about 1/2 an hour to paint a picture of what was going down at Stella's Tavern and to assure our Lieutenant that we were ready to make it work. Whitehead informed us that arrangements had already been made with District 12 to keep patrol cars a couple of blocks away from the local bar on Western Avenue and to be on standby if needed. So, he had already made up his mind. I guess he just wanted to hear it from us.

We signed out a Chevy Impala sedan for the day and decided that Elaina would take it to meet up with Agent Marek at the FBI, and I would take Paige's car to the Ukrainian village to hook up with Tony Wright. On the way out, the team exchanged some handshakes and high-fives while telling each other to watch our backs and be safe.

Out in the parking lot I went over some details with Elaine one more time. She and Teresa Marek would have their service weapons in their bags, and they would both be wearing wires that could pick up sound, but they would not be able to communicate directly to us in the sound truck. But since everyone is constantly on their phones these days, we could exchange texts without raising any suspicion.

On my way to Ukrainian Village driving Paige's car, it made me want to hear her voice. When I called her, I had to settle for her greeting on voicemail. Not what I was hoping for, but better than nothing. So, I left a message promising to contact her later, as soon as our operation was completed.

The city was very alive on this sunny Saturday morning. North Avenue was bustling with shoppers and people beginning to file into the many restaurants and pubs located in Old Town and then Wicker Park. When I reached Western Avenue, I turned left going south toward Ukrainian Village. Stella's is just past Augusta Boulevard on the left. So, a couple of blocks before that I turned left on W. Cortez St. and then took a series of right turns before finding the FBI van on W. Walton St. about two blocks away from Stella's Tap.

The instructions were to look for a white van marked with black block lettering promoting the Ace Painting Company with a prominent depiction of the ace of spades on both sides of the vehicle.

When I pulled into a spot on the street a few spaces behind the van, there was light traffic and a few pedestrians at the end of the block. Apparently, Agent Wright had spotted me, because my phone buzzed right away. He told me to wait for a lull in the car and foot traffic and then to walk to the back of the truck and get right in, when the doors opened.

Within a couple of minutes Walnut Street was completely clear. I got out of the car and walked directly down the sidewalk to the back of the Ace Painting Company van. The doors swung open and I hopped in, before Tony Wright immediately closed them behind me. In the front there was an amazing panel of sound and video equipment and a guy sitting in a swivel desk chair. There were two other smaller swivel chairs on either side of the van. All three of the chairs could turn 360°, but were bolted to the floor. Tony introduced me to our technical sound specialist, Special Agent Wilbur Jones. He was a short slender guy with bright blue eyes and short cropped blonde hair. I figured him to be even younger than me somewhere in his mid to late 20s. Both he and Tony were wearing painting pants and short-sleeved white shirts with block lettering saying Ace Painting Company. I was handed my own work uniform and quickly put it on.

Agent Jones took over the meeting and proceeded to showcase all of the sound and video equipment capabilities. There were four small video screens in front of him which covered feeds from all sides of the van. In cases, where they were able to plant cameras inside of a building, they could get the video on those screens. But there was no time to do that in this case.

The sound system, however, would be the focus this operation. The outside of the truck was wired with thin antenna wires that were virtually invisible to the naked eye. The sound wires that Elaina and Teresa were going to wear inside the bar would be able to pick up sounds within about 10 to 15 feet of them and would be fed into different radio signals so as not to interfere with each other. Teresa would also be equipped with a sound bug implanted in a small wad of sticky substance that looked like gum. As soon as the targets chose a table or booth she would try to plant it near them. That feed would go to a third channel.

Since the meeting was scheduled for 3 PM, our plan was to wait until around 2 PM before finding a parking spot on Western Avenue within 150 feet of Stella's. They had already checked the equipment out and determined that a parking spot north of the bar on the same side of the street was optimal for the sound transmission. Until then, we would pick up some sandwiches at the 7-Eleven on N. Damon in Wicker Park and make sure we used a bathroom before settling in for who knows how long near Stella's Tap.

At around 1:30 PM I got a text from Elaina stating that she and Teresa were on schedule and were already dressed and wired up for their trip to the bar. They would both have pistols in their purses, and Teresa was ready with a couple of sound bugs to place near the targets if she got the opportunity.

By 2 PM Morgan Latner and Henrique Sanchez were positioned on a side street north of Stella's while Zileen Baker and George Makris were on a street south of the place.

At 2:20 PM the camera monitor in front of our truck picked up Elaina and Teresa walking toward us on the sidewalk. I couldn't help thinking that they really looked the part. Teresa Marek with her shoulder length light brown hair let down and wearing a white tank top and tight jeans cut quite an attractive figure. And Elaina, wearing her brown hair tied up with a cowgirl hat on top, a light blue tank top and formfitting jeans, was equally hot.

"The regulars at Stella's are going to love them." I said with a laugh. Agent Tony Wright chuckled too and added that he hoped the targets were too distracted to be suspicious. Once they got inside, we could hear the detective and agent greeting Rita at the bar and ordering light beers. I was wearing the headset that picked up Elaina's feed and Tony was receiving Teresa's. I could tell that the bar was quiet at that time, and Elaina texted me confirming that. It was now a matter of waiting for some lowlife anarchists and Russian gangsters to show up.

By 3:30 PM no one that we were interested in had shown up. The ladies had managed to nurse a couple of beers each, while winning several games of pool against some of the regulars. They had also managed to fend off a number of offers for shots, but the boys were getting more persistent and the bar was starting to fill up and get livelier. The jukebox was a constant, and clearly hearing Elaina's voice was getting more and more difficult.

At 4 PM we were all getting worried. I texted my partner to ask how they were doing in there. She responded they were fine, but they had lost their last game of pool and had to give up the table to some of the locals. They were now trapped at the bar and were feeling that not taking a shot was drawing more attention to them than it was worth. I knew that Elaina could hold her liquor, so I told her to go ahead. And just then I spotted two men approaching from the south wearing baseball caps, long sleeve denim shirts and jeans. I then saw that there were two other guys with shaved heads wearing white short-sleeved button-down shirts and dark pants approaching from the north.

Here were our targets. The Russians from the north and the fanatics from the south. They stopped in front of Stella's door and walked in together. I quickly texted Elaina while Tony was contacting Agent Marek. My partner responded that she had it covered and would keep in touch.

For the next 10 minutes the only things that I heard from Elaina's feed were songs on the jukebox, snippets of conversations and the occasional cracking of pool table balls colliding together. Then Elaina's voice came through clearly ."Would any of you boys like to take us on. In a game of pool that is." She said laughingly.

"No thanks sweetheart." One of the First Patriots responded.

"Are you sure? We really know how to play. We're good at pool too." This time it was the voice of Teresa Marek.

"I said no. Now move on. Go play with someone else or play with yourselves."

Then I could hear something coming from one of the Russians, but it was muffled and I wouldn't have understood it anyway. Elaina said something to them along the lines of it being their loss, and then the sound went back to being a chaotic blend of music and voices.

In the front of the van, I noticed sound technician Wilbur Jones spin around in his chair to face the console which now was showing a blinking red light. He put on some head phones and started waving at Tony Wright and manipulating dials on the console. "We have transmission from one of Marek's bugs!" he exclaimed excitedly.

Then Agent Wright looked down at his phone and informed us that Teresa Marek had just confirmed that she was able to place a listening device on the side of the targets' booth. She also noted that the Russians had called the First Patriot guys low class morons while smiling at them.

You can't make the shit up, I thought to myself. I also was thinking that maybe we should pull our partners out of Stella's. But when I suggested it to Elaina, she objected. She said that they wanted to stay until the targets end their meeting, just in case something went wrong with the first bug.

Tony Wright and I resigned ourselves to the fact that our partners were dug in and not coming out until the meeting was over. Once again, I was encouraged by the fact that Elaina could drink most guys including me under the table, on the rare occasion when she chose to. And I was amused by the thought of the local boys making a run at our two attractive pool playing partners.

Wilbur Jones began giving us a play-by-play account of the conversations at the booth. It was being recorded, but we appreciated getting it in real time. And he reported everything. As it turned out, Agent Jones was a linguist and spoke fluent Russian.

The information coming from those guys was incredibly revealing and disturbing. Both the container ships carrying stolen vehicles had reached their destinations in Venezuela and Cuba on

Thursday. The money from Venezuela had been transferred to an account in the US controlled by the Dixie Mafia who were to take their cut before releasing the bulk of the funds to the Russians, after the shipment from Cuba was delivered to the First Patriots on Sunday night.

The Russians were clearly unhappy with this arrangement, but there was nothing they could do about it, because the Dixie Mafia was aligned with the lowlife morons. They would have to settle for being present, when the military hardware was delivered to an abandoned warehouse in Norridge. This was a change in plans and the Russians insisted on expressing that they didn't trust the Chicago PD detectives who had pushed for the delivery to be carried out at the former bus depot in Jefferson Park.

The First Patriots agreed to the switch, but assured the Russians that the Chicago detectives wouldn't be a problem. They were trying to squeeze them for more money to protect the exchange in Jefferson Park. They said that their man, Lester Shelton, was going to meet them at the old bus depot Sunday night at 10 PM and take care of the problem, while the goods would be delivered in Norridge at midnight. They assured the Russians that N.O. wouldn't bother them anymore.

One of the Russians asked why Lester Shelton wasn't at their meeting and was told that he had other business to take care of that day. They laughed and said that after Shelton took out the dirty cops, he would disappear for a while and then come back when the First Patriots were ready to carry out an armed attack on key government buildings and institutions in Chicago hoping to spark a race war that would be led by them and result in a total societal breakdown.

With that, the nefarious meeting came to a close. They wished each other luck in English, promising to meet up at midnight the next day in Norridge. Then Wilbur Jones began laughing nearly hysterically, while struggling to report that the Russians had just shook hands with the First Patriots and said something in Russian causing them to express thanks. The Russians had told them to go fuck themselves and take their mothers with them. What a great bunch.

We watched the odd couples exit Stella's and go their separate ways. All of us felt good that we were able to get important intelligence on the final leg of their ambitious auto theft for big money from Venezuela and high end weapons from Cuba plans. Elaina texted that she and Teresa were going to stay for a short time to finish their last game of pool and retrieve the listening device.

I noticed that it was already 5:45 PM, and Paige would need a ride from the State's Attorney's Office. Before I could place a call to her, my phone buzzed with a call from Paige. But when I answered, it wasn't her voice that I heard.

"Jack this is Tara Thistle. I am at Paige's apartment building. I took her here after work to pick up some clothes and mail. When we got here, she asked me to run over to the Walgreens around the corner to get her some feminine products. Jack, I was only gone for five minutes. I swear. I just got back and she's not responding to the doorbell. I went to the back door, and it's locked but one of the glass panels is broken. You need to get here right now!"

"I'm on my way! Call 911 for police and ambulance. I have keys to the apartment. God dammit Tara, what the hell were you thinking!"

I was jolted into action. There was no time to let panic set in. Wilbur Jones jumped into the driver's seat and pulled onto Western Avenue, took the first right and went two blocks to the silver Honda, I was driving. I bolted out and into the vehicle. Fortunately, I was only a couple of miles from the apartment and driving with reckless abandon, I made it there in five minutes.

When I arrived, EMTs were standing on the sidewalk outside the front entrance. Racing past them I opened the vestibule door and bounded up the stairs to the second-floor apartment. Inside, there were signs of a violent struggle in the front room, where the coffee table was turned over and lamps and artwork were scattered on the floor. A blood trail led through the narrow hallway past the bathroom and into Paige's bedroom. What I found there stopped me dead in my tracks and took my breath away.

Paige was laid out halfway onto her bed in a pool of blood that soaked the bedspread and her once white blouse. Her lifeless dark brown eyes were staring up to the ceiling and there was a long pearl handled knife sticking straight up out of her throat. My legs gave out and I fell to my knees in front of her on the floor. The EMTs rushed past me and began taking her vital signs and looking for signs of life, signs of hope. There weren't any. I couldn't speak, even though I wanted to scream. I couldn't cry, even though I desperately needed to. I couldn't feel anything, no matter how much I wanted to.

I just stood up, pulled the white handle stiletto from Paige's neck, folded it and put it in my pocket. There was no thought about evidence or police procedure. I knew what I needed to do, and where the knife needed to be.

Chapter 25

I walked through the hallway and into the kitchen. I could see glass on the floor and the broken window pane in the back door. To my surprise, the door wasn't locked, as Tara Thistle had reported. I walked out to the second-floor landing expecting to see her sitting out there in a state of panic. But she was nowhere to be seen.

A rush of anger swept over me. She had led Paige to her death. That bitch was one of them. She was one of those god damn racist freaks. She was the TT that Victor Kirilenko was talking about. She wouldn't be dumb enough to go home. I would deal with her later. I had a plan, and I needed to keep my focus.

I was glad to be feeling something, but with torrid anger replacing frigid emptiness it seemed like my equilibrium was turned upside down. I was nearly getting to the point, where I couldn't breathe. In my dazed state Paige's car fairly found its own way to Uptown and parked itself in front of the Green Mill.

When I got out of the car, a stiff northerly breeze hit me in the face and snapped me out of my trance like state a little bit. Inside there was a sparse crowd gathering, before the music started, and the late night people arrived. It was good to see Gus Kezios behind the bar, and he brought me over a Miller High Life and a shot of Jack Daniels and poured one for himself.

"I can see that you need this. You look terrible Jack."

"Nice to see you too Gus." I responded.

We clinked shot glasses together and bolted them down followed by another. I gave him a very general idea of how my day had gone, but couldn't talk about Paige. He hadn't known her, and I didn't want to confront the reality of it. So, I concentrated on my beers, and Gus got busy with other customers.

My mind was racing and formulating the details of the plan that crossed my mind, the minute I saw Paige lying there with Lester Shelton's stiletto protruding from her beautiful neck. The first thing I decided to do was get in touch with Dominic Blasi, the young financial advisor that I had saved from a couple of ninja assassins out on Lake Michigan earlier that summer. I needed a favor, and I figured he owed me one.

I had Blasi's cell phone number in my contact list, and after pressing call, I soon heard his voice on the other end. He was surprised that I called, but picked up on the seriousness of my reason right away. I wanted him to set up a meeting for me with his uncle, the guy from River Forest that Dominic had said knew how to handle difficult situations. He quickly understood what I needed, and that I needed it right away. He promised to get back to me that night.

Gus brought me another Miller and a notice flashed that a text had come in. I open my messages and saw that it was Elaina, and that there were two other messages from her and one from my dad and another from my best friend, Morgan Latner. They all knew about Paige, and they were all worried about me. I didn't want to respond to any of them, but I knew that I needed to touch base with my partner. Otherwise, she would have driven to Uptown looking for me.

So I messaged back to Elaina that I was okay and would need a little time. I asked her to plan on coordinating with Agents Wright and Marek on intercepting the weapons delivery in Norridge late Sunday night. We would deal with the other players in this case, after the Russians and First Patriots were rounded up with the Cuban weapons. Until then, we needed to keep the Chicago PD out of it. She agreed, but made me promise to take care of myself and stay in touch. So, I lied and said that I would.

Gus delivered yet another Miller just as my buddy, Morgan, sat down beside me. "Hey Jack, I would ask you how you were doing, but you look like hell, so I won't bother."

We knew each other so well. His dry sense of humor usually made me laugh, but not this time. My total lack of reaction brought a real look of worry to his face.

"I'm so sorry man. I really wish, there were something that I could do. Anything you need. I got you."

"I know you do. Don't think I don't appreciate it. Thanks for seeking me out. But this is going to take some time. Some real time. I just need some space for a while to find my way out."

I wasn't about to tell them what was on my mind. Just like Elaina he would have tried to talk me out of it and then tried to help me with it, if that failed. I didn't want either of those things to happen. Their lives and careers would not be jeopardized out of loyalty to me. This was my path to travel alone.

Morgan stayed for a couple of beers, and we did our best to have a normal conversation about the Cubs whose season was winding down and the Bears who were just getting started. Such discussions usually inspired enthusiasm and good-natured arguments between us, but we were both just going through the motions. When he finished his second beer, we both stood up, and he gave me a warm hug. I could feel his worry and concern. But I couldn't feel any of my own emotions. I hoped that by the next time I saw him, I could.

At around 11 PM Dominic Blasi called back and informed me that his uncle, John Torchio had agreed to meet with me at noon the next day, after he was done with Sunday Mass and breakfast with his family. I was to meet him at an establishment that he owned in Forest Park called Roma's. It was a little neighborhood bar just off Roosevelt Road that I had heard of but never frequented.

I thanked Blasi, and he told me that we were even for me saving his life, when I threw him overboard from a dinner cruise on Lake Michigan in June. He laughed and reminded me that I still owed him a sport coat on that deal. I couldn't help thinking that if I was able to get through the next few days, I would get him his sport coat.

When I was about to leave the Green Mill around midnight, Gus called me back to the bar. "Hey Jack, I almost forgot that Emma left this note for you a couple of days ago. She's back from that artist retreat in Arizona."

I opened the colorful homemade note card and read a nice greeting and a request to call her with her phone number. What the fuck, I thought. Only a few weeks earlier I would have been thrilled to have Emma Merlin reach out to me and offer me her phone number. Now, I put the note in my pocket and walked out into the storms that were raging in my life.

As soon as I was out the door of the Green Mill, I was greeted by an explosive clap of thunder followed closely by a mammoth flash of lightning to the east. Rain was pounding the sidewalk and street, and the wind was whipping around violently pushing the rain sideways at times. By the time I reached the car I was already drenched. Feeling drawn to the lightning, I drove directly to Montrose Beach and parked as close to the lake as possible.

The powerful thunderous sounds and closeness of the long tentacled streaks of lightning somehow was calming to me. It wasn't a sense of pleasure, as storms had provided me in the past, but more of an escape momentarily from the depths of my pain and rage.

I don't know how long the banging and light show continued out over Lake Michigan. Time wasn't recognizable to me. It was neither moving forward or standing still. It was stuck somewhere inside me, desperately trying to find a way out.

The rain continued pouring down, but the wind had calmed, and the water was no longer visible. Everything went dark. One of my father's favorite songs crept into my head, and it kept playing over and over in my mind, until mercifully I found temporary escape in sleep. My lullaby was Brook Benton's rendition of Rainy Night in Georgia. 'Heavy rains fallin' seems I hear your voice callin' it's all right. A rainy night in Georgia. Lord, I believe it's rainin' all over the world.'

When I awoke, it was daylight, but there was no sun. The rain had stopped, but the skies were dark and menacing. Even the lake seemed angry, as its high waves came crashing onto the shore with heavy winds at their back. The temperature was a good 30° colder than the day before, but none of this meant anything to me.

The only reason that I knew it was Sunday, was because my meeting with John Torchio was scheduled after he and his family returned from Mass. I dreaded going back to my apartment, but I needed to clean up and show some respect to Dominic Blasi's uncle.

Everything about my home made me uncomfortable. I was driving Paige's car, and wherever I looked in the apartment reminded me of her. The most surreal part of being there was taking a shower where we had spent some of our most intimate moments. Every time I closed my eyes to put my head under the water, I could feel her arms around me and her lips on the back of my neck. When I pulled my head out from under the shower, it was like waking from a wonderful dream and realizing that it wasn't real, and that reality was something completely different.

I had no appetite and didn't want to watch television or listen to music. Any kind of stimulation would have caused an even higher level of anxiety. I couldn't afford to be paralyzed with depression. I was on a mission and needed a cold steely focus.

When it came time to leave for my meeting, I had shaved, showered and donned a sharp navy blue suit with a light blue Oxford shirt and black Rockport work shoes. I looked pretty good and felt pretty damn lousy.

I drove down Lakeshore Drive paying little attention to the gloomy day and roiling lake to my left. I got off at Erie Street and took Ontario Street to the Eisenhower Expressway for the ride to the Forest Park exit at Harlem Avenue. A few minutes later I pulled up just past Roma's Bar. It was dark and didn't seem to be open.

When as I got out of the car, a very large serious looking guy walked out of the front door and led me into Roma's without saying a word and without frisking me. We walked past the bar and stopped, when we got to a closed door, he told me to go right in. Mr. Torchio was expecting me.

I gingerly opened the door and slowly walked into the spacious dark room, illuminated only by an antique lamp sitting atop a large mahogany desk flanked by two dark leather easy chairs. He was standing in front of the desk and greeted me with a hug and kiss on the cheek. He then motioned for me to sit and walked around the desk to his large leather swivel chair.

"Thank you for agreeing to see me Mr. Torchio." I said earnestly.

"Please call me John. Consider yourself a friend of my family. What you did for my nephew Dominic will not be forgotten. Dom has always been my wife's favorite nephew. She sends her gratitude. Of course, she doesn't know anything about why you are here. I, however, understand these things. I am happy to do you this favor."

"Yes, I completely understand, Jack. These people you talk about. We know them. The Russians are animals, but in the end you can do business with them. These other guys are worthless bums. They aren't really interested in business. They only hate and want to tear down everything. We don't normally interfere with other people's business, you understand. But we won't cry, if they go away.

Torchio reached into the bottom drawer of his desk and pulled out a purple silky looking pouch with gold drawstrings. He handed it to me. "Everything you need is in this little sack. Remember to leave the gun and take the sack and gloves. Be careful. Good luck Jack."

He stood up and came around the desk and gave me another hug and a kiss on both cheeks this time. John Torchio walked me out of his office and as far as the front door, before handing me off to the large gray suited guy who escorted me to my car.

I got in and placed the purple pouch on the passenger seat and breathed a sigh of relief. Before yesterday I would never have imagined that I'd be asking for a favor from one of the Chicago Outfit's main men, and much less that he would have entertained it. But none of that really mattered much to me. I had a mission to accomplish.

My appetite had not returned, but I knew that I had to eat something. Thinking about what would be appealing to me in my current condition, I immediately thought of one of my go to favorites since my high school years. I knew that an Italian Beef sandwich from Johnnie's in Elmwood Park would do the trick.

So, I started up the CRV and drove a few blocks east to Harlem Avenue and turned left. A couple of miles north I turned left again on North Avenue and three blocks up on the right, there it was. Johnnie's always seemed to be busy, but on this day it wasn't too bad.

After waiting for about five minutes to get to the counter, I ordered a large beef with onions, sweet peppers and giardiniera. I like mine baptized with fries and a Coke. I took it to the counter along the windows and did my best to get this delicious soaked sandwich down, without making a complete mess out of my navy blue suit.

The tactic of going with one of my favorite foods along with the much-needed nutrition helped me feel almost alive. I knew that it was a necessary part, of what I needed to do that day. But there was no time to savor the experience. I needed to go back to my apartment to try to get some rest. I was still wired, but a feeling of exhaustion was starting to set in.

Back home I quickly changed out of my suit and put on a pair of jeans and a sweatshirt, before laying down on the couch. I set the alarm on my phone and fell asleep, almost as soon as my head hit the couch pillow.

The alarm sounded, while I was still experiencing a deep sleep and dreaming of being with Paige in some unrecognizable place. It started out with us walking along a quiet street holding hands and laughing. Then she said that she needed to go into the apartment to get her phone. She would only be a minute. But, she never came back out and I went in looking for her but she wasn't there. She wasn't anywhere.

When I was fully awake, I was glad to realize that it had only been a dream, but the relief didn't last long, because the reality was much worse.

Darkness had fallen, and the rain returned at a pretty strong rate. I put on a black baseball cap and charcoal gray waterproof windbreaker along with a pair of black waterproof walking shoes. When it got to be 8 PM, I couldn't wait any longer. The corrupt Chicago cops were due to be at the abandoned bus garage in Jefferson Park at 10 PM, and I figured Lester Shelton would want to be there well ahead of them. So, I wanted to get there by 8:30 PM.

On the drive there I mulled over some of the questions that had been answered in the case and others that had not. We now knew the scope of the general goal of the carjacking partnership between the unlikely co-conspirators. The Russians recognized the opportunity to use a group that they saw as ignorant lowlifes for a quick multi-million dollar score, and the First Patriots who didn't really know anything about the Russians or anything else, saw a chance to get a cache of sophisticated military weapons that they could use to wreak havoc on the governmental and legal structure of Chicago, hoping to cause a type of racial Civil War.

I felt strongly that the person that Victor Kirilenko was referring to in the State's Attorney's Office, was actually Tara Thistle and not Terrance Timothy Goggins. As big of a jerk that Goggins was, it was Tara Thistle that led Paige to the slaughter and then disappeared.

The FBI had uncovered that Detective Oscar Anderson had changed his name from Nikita Orlov. So, that seemed to indicate that he was the Chicago PD member Kirilenko referred to as N.O. And who had been working with the Russians and First Patriots. I was expecting to see him and his partner Jorge Solar soon.

The former bus garage was located in a fairly large industrial area with some warehouses and light manufacturing operations that were either shut down or only partially operating. I had been there before, but it had been a while. When I got a couple of blocks away, I parked behind an abandoned manufacturing plant. I didn't see any cameras, but it was always safe to assume that there could be some, so I chose the darkest area to park Paige's silver CRV. I placed the purple sack in my deep windbreaker pocket and was carrying Lester Shelton stiletto in my hip pocket.

I zipped up my jacket, put the hood up over the black baseball cap and stepped out into the rain. The walk to the old bus garage was largely through the industrial section and brought me to the back of the large former bus garage. There was only one door leading inside that I could see. I approached carefully and stopped about 50 yards away before slowly going closer, moving behind a large dumpster that was located to the right of the door which had a punch in keypad.

The rain continued to be steady, and there was virtually no lighting other than a dim light in a nearby alley that barely made a dent in the darkness. I had a good vantage point from behind the dumpster which blocked me from being seen by anyone pulling in from the alley, but allowed me a clear view of the door.

Standing there in the darkness and rain was sort of surreal. I tried not to think about Paige or anything else other than taking care of the business that brought me there. I also was trying to get the Brook Benton song out of my head. But, it just kept coming back, so I gave up and just went with it.

"late at night when it's hard to rest I hold your picture to my chest and I feel fine"

Then the bright headlights of a truck snapped me out of it. I crouched down, until the lights went off, and a door opened and then slammed shut. My eyes were fixed on the door to the building and then the unmistakable figure of Lester Shelton standing in front of it punching in the access code.

I moveed slowly around the dumpster and the rain completely muffled any sound from my footsteps. I reached into my hip pocket for the stiletto and opened the blade. Just as Shelton turned the handle and opened the door, I thrust the knife into his back just under his rib cage and into his liver. He gasped and started to slump. I pulled the blade out and turned him around while holding him up and sticking my foot inside the door.

I wanted him to look me in the eye and know who was killing him. The expression of terror on his face was all I needed to see. There was no need to say anything. The next thrust went between his ribs and straight into his black heart. He groaned one last time and shuddered before going completely limp.

He crumpled into the doorway, and I left him there, while I looked for something to keep the door propped open. Looking around the area I noticed a small pile of red Chicago bricks and brought one over to the doorway. After dragging Shelton out onto the wet ground, I was happy to see that the brick held, working as a door jam. I then dragged the bastard over to the dumpster like a big bag of garbage. I threw the lid open and picked up Shelton and managed to lift him up to the lip of the container, flip him over the side into the trash where he belonged and close the lid.

I threw the brick to the side and entered into the totally darkened cavernous space. I pulled out my cell phone which had already been muted. I used the flashlight to provide some illumination, revealing a small office which protruded out from the wall to my right.

There was a small window on the side nearest me and a door opening out into the body of the huge garage. I put on the surgical gloves, before trying the door. It was open. So, I went in and flipped a switch on the wall which turned on a ceiling light and then immediately turned it back off.

I sat down in a small swivel chair behind a simple metal desk and took out the purple satchel and opened it up. I removed the 38 Caliber revolver and inspected it. It was ready to go. I placed it on the desk and checked my phone. It was already 9:45 and time to be on high alert. A text popped up from Elaina asking where I was and informing me that the bodies of Detectives Oscar Anderson and Jorge Solar had just been pulled out of Lake Michigan at Monroe Harbor. She didn't have any more information. She was with the FBI preparing to bust the First Patriots and Russians, when the Cuban weapons were delivered in Norridge.

That news really had my mind racing. It meant that the First Patriots had already eliminated the N.O. that Kirilenko was referring to. But then what the hell was Lester Shelton doing there? I didn't have long to think about it before there was sound coming from the door and footsteps on the concrete. Tap tap tap. The sound kept getting closer.

I saw two shadowy figures pass by the window and then the door opened and the light came on. I'll be damned I thought. It was Detectives Carl Nijinsky and Roger O'Brien. They were the fucking N.O.!

Bam! Bam! My shots rang out. It only took two. They both fell to the floor with bullet holes in their foreheads.

I coldly stood up and dropped the gun on the desk and put the purple pouch in my coat pocket. I stepped over the dead bodies, turned off the light and closed the door on two dirty detectives and the only job that I had ever wanted.

Epilogue

Monday morning I slept soundly until 10 AM. I didn't bother calling in to the station or even checking the duty schedule. I wasn't planning on going in that day either way. Then I started checking my texts and came across a message from Elaina, asking how I was doing, and whether I was enjoying a day off. There were others from her and my buddy Morgan Latner. I would have to respond to them later.

The rain had stopped over night, and the sun was shining brightly in a nearly cloudless sky. Life was going on for more than 2 1/2 million Chicagoans, but I was having a tough time going along with it.

After hanging around my apartment for several hours, I found the initiative to give my partner a call. She seemed relieved to hear from me and said she was worried sick about me and was so sorry about Paige. She also informed me about how the bust in Norridge went down.

Elaina had accompanied Teresa Marek and Tony Wright along with a dozen fellow FBI agents and more agents from the Bureau of Alcohol, Tobacco, Firearms and Explosives. They caught the carjacking conspirators red-handed with a huge arsenal of military weapons which included automatic rifles, small artillery and rocket launchers.

They arrested a dozen Russian gangsters and nearly 20 First Patriots. Unsurprisingly, the Russians didn't say anything. They wouldn't even identify themselves. The First Patriots however, were a different story. Several of them, including one of the guys who attended the meeting at Stella's, broke down right away. He confessed to the whole plan and gave up Tara Thistle as a dedicated member of their group. She had steered the State's Attorney's Office away from the white supremacist organization and paid off the corrupt detectives, Carl Nijinsky and Roger O'Brien.

He gave up Lester Shelton and Tara Thistle as the perpetrators of Paige's murder and the plan to have Lester Shelton take out Detectives Nijinsky and O'Brien in Jefferson Park rather than pay them more money. All this apparently led the FBI to believe that Shelton was responsible for gunning down the detectives before the Russians decided to eliminate him as a dangerous lose cannon that could lead the police to them. As it turned out, Terrance Timothy Goggins had nothing to do with the First Patriots. He was just an unscrupulous overly ambitious prosecutor without a conscience.

I thanked Elaina for checking in on me and told her that I had been home since late Saturday night and just not answering any calls or texts. She urged me to take care of myself and said she would see me at the station the next day.

When the next day arrived, I awoke feeling somewhat rested but cold and numb inside. I drove into the Chicago PD station on N. Larrabee St. that had been the focal point of my life for nearly the past four years. I had managed to shave and clean myself up, so when I walked into the detectives' room no one batted an eye.

The room was buzzing with chatter about the huge bust in Norridge and the murder of Detectives Carl Nijinsky and Roger O'Brien. One by one the team members, Zileen Baker, George Makris, Henrique Sanchez, Morgan Latner and lastly my partner, Elaina Rodriguez came by to express condolences and sincere offers to help me out in any way.

I appreciated everyone in that room, but it was difficult to feel much of anything. Other than calling the ME's office on Monday to check on the status of Paige's autopsy, I couldn't get myself to think about her death. I did learn that her parents had been notified and were already in Chicago to take charge of their daughter's funeral arrangements. I never got a chance to meet them, and I wondered whether I ever would.

Everybody was busy working on other cases. The cases never stop coming in. I didn't ever really dwell on that. I just jumped right in and loved every minute of it. Elaina was engrossed in something on her computer screen, when I tapped her on the shoulder and asked her to come with me to a conference room. There I told her of what I was about to do, and her jaw dropped.

"Oh Dios min Jack. Are you sure that is what you want to do? What you need to do?"

I assured her that it was. I couldn't tell her about what I had done. She and Morgan were better off not knowing. They would continue to believe that it was an emotional response to losing Paige the way I did. It wasn't far from the truth anyway.

Elaina stood up with tears welling up in her eyes and hugged me warmly. I couldn't say anything else and turned walking out of the room directly to Lieutenant Whitehead's office. I placed my detective's Star on his desk. They already had my Beretta from the shooting on North Avenue.

Whitehead knew immediately what I was doing and tried to find out, if there was anything he could do for me that would change my mind. After about 15 minutes he realized that my decision was firm and got up and shook my hand and wished me well.

I walked directly out to the street and started walking and didn't stop, until I walked all the way home. The key fob was left in Paige's car. I would make sure that her parents were informed of its whereabouts. My Camaro wouldn't be ready from the body shop for a while, but I could get along in Chicago just fine without it.

My future was murky at best. I wasn't sure about anything. I had some savings and had accrued seven years of pension benefits that I could cash in. I would be okay for a while anyway.

The note from Emma Merlin that Gus Kezios passed on to me at the Green Mill was sitting on top of my dresser. I knew that there would come a day, when I would get through the hurt and figure things out. When that day came, I also knew that I would be calling Emma. But, it was not that day.